I AM RAHAB: A Novel
by JC Miller

I AM RAHAB

Dedicated to Mommy, I miss you.

J.C. MILLER

Table of Contents

J.C. MILLER

ISBN: 978-1-7339386-0-0 (Paperback)
Library of Congress Control Number: 2019907491

Any references to historical events, real people, or real places are used fictitiously. Names, characters, and places are products of the author's imagination.

Book Graphic Design Chanel Smith, WPD Media LLC

Editing Tiya Marshall, Marshall Editing and Consulting

Printed in the United States of America.

First printing edition 2019.
Jess, Mo' Books
P.O. Bx. 1808
Albrightsville, PA. 18210
JessMoBooksLLC.Wixsite.com/jmbllc

Introduction

This is a fictional family saga covering the lives of four generations of Auguste women. This timeless tale is based upon the biblical encounter of Rahab the Harlot, cleverly set in the 20th century, and parallels the biblical account of sin, redemption, faith, love, and grace. *I AM RAHAB: A Novel, by JC Miller,* intertwines the lives of several characters seen throughout the Bible and pits them against modern setbacks.

I AM RAHAB

PART ONE

PROLOGUE

"What do you see?"
I said, "I see a boiling caldron; and it is tipping away from
the north."
Jeremiah 1:13

If it is possible to smell death, Rahab can smell it on Jeremy. The foul odor passes through his pores and ripples from his breath.

"Why, Rah? Why?" he shouts over her silent terror. But she can't speak. There's nothing to say; her words can't undo what's already been said. She's his captive, yet she's aware that she's more than a prisoner.

Jeremy's mind screams for him to *surrender, raise the white flag!* But prison isn't an option. *Yo! Players don't go out like that. They go out HARD.* His sanity debates with the sense of insanity gripping him. Rahab's trembling body held against his alerts him; *it's not about the game anymore. She's involved* He releases a sigh of despair.

"I love you," he reluctantly confesses; three words he's never uttered before. He then plants a sloppy wet kiss on her forehead. "If this is it...it's gonna be you and me forever, *Bonnie* and *Clyde* style," he concludes, drawing Rahab closer as though trying to consume her. His trembling hand tightly grips the gun he is pressing against her temple.

Click. Jeremy cocks the pistol, ignoring the pleas from those in the room. All he can hear is his own heavy breathing. *I always hated the way that movie ends.* Remembering Bonnie and Clyde were killed in cold blood,

Jeremy prefers to hold his and Rahab's destinies in his hands.

At that moment, time stands still. Rahab's family, helplessly watching the ordeal, freeze. Their stone-like faces grimace in agony. Rahab's tears stop flowing and become plastered to her face. She can't move; her body is stiff. From the corner of her eye, she looks up at Jeremy. His eyes, frozen upon her, have lost their intensity. He doesn't look like himself, and he seems conflicted, an inner war plays on his long face. Rahab's body becomes numb as a calming peace washes over her. She closes her eyes and gives everything she has to Him, the Lord.

BANG! The gun fires.

From her mind's eye, Rahab can see her grandmother, Big Mama, boiling sheets. She sees herself, young and innocent, underfoot. She can feel the warmth of the hot steam coming up from the boiling pot.

Am I dead?

J.C. MILLER

LOTTI

PEDDLING A BLUE-EYED GOD

Charlotte Auguste, known as Lotti or Big Mama to friends and family, grew up in Baton Rouge, all along the Mississippi River. She was raised by her grandmother, a baby-catcher (midwife), and Voodoo priestess. The Auguste women are Louisiana Creole mostly of Haitian descent. The passing down of their proud heritage and Voodoo traditions is customary. Lotti learned about gris-gris bags, hexes, and charms right along with the alphabet and arithmetic. It's no surprise that she meddles in the underworld of elixirs, oils, and potions, yet she doesn't consider it witchcraft, or Voodoo.

"I'm a businesswoman and a spiritual guide," Lotti insists to others.

She manages her trades from home. Besides boiling sheets in her signature scent, she's a midwife by day and takes lives by night aborting babies. She dabbles in pharmaceutical practices, selling her herbed remedies to those seeking *alternative medicine.* Lotti also gives spiritual advice and, every now and then, casts a spell or two. Most would call her lifestyle unsavory, but she does what she knows how to survive.

As children, Lotti and her younger sister, Mary Magdalene, affectionately known as Mags, moved often with their grandmother who raised them after their mother passed during childbirth. In every town they lived in, the townspeople felt their grandmother's Voodoo harbored evil spirits and caused calamity over them. The truth was, everything that could go wrong went wrong when she was around.

Yes, *The Grandmother,* as Lotti and Mags lovingly referred to her, a short, sassy, white-haired woman who stood high on pride, had an evil streak. She was stubborn to a fault and only moved when the spirits moved her, but she wasn't a troublemaker. In the 1930s and 40s, before its popularity with tourists, Voodoo and black magic was pushed into the darkness of the swamps. No matter where the family moved, their grandmother never met approval, especially amongst the church.

But the church always fascinated Lotti. The Grandmother taught her to be self-reliant so she never leaned on faith. She used Voodoo and spirituality as a means of income. Lotti didn't practice dark magic nor religion. She lived simply, made her own rules and minded her business. But the church seemed to stir itself up in her life.

Lotti often spoke of a classmate extending her an invitation to a tent revival. She remembered listening in wonderment as people received deliverance from the Lord and often shared with her own granddaughter, Rahab, about the experience.

"Dey gave dey money as an offering, and when dey was healed dey gave more money. It was right der ah learned, dem pastors is de real witch doctors. Making folk see what dey want dem to see and do what dey want dem to do, all in de name of some blue-eyed white god dey peddling. Naw you know how Big Mama loves her some money. Dey turned me into a believer, too, ah guarantee!"

Lotti's classmate, who extended the invitation, later snuck her a Bible.

"Fuh years, ah read dat book until de words fixed to me. Ah wanted to be a part of de love dat was in it, but de world wouldn't let me in. We was different, all we knew was Voodoo and all we had was each other. As ah got older and was needed to help out with money in de house, ah decided, if de preacher could sell his god, so could ah. Ah bottled some remedies, notions, and potions and started selling dem on de other side of de river. Ah told folks Jesus came to me in a dream and revealed how to heal his people. Dey fell fuh it hook, line, and sinker, too," Lotti laughed. "Mags tagged along. She was my guinea pig in need of healing. Ah cured her of leprosy, migraines, being crippled, deaf, and blind. Boy, we had us a time fuh sho," Lotti joyfully explained.

For nearly a year, the sisters worked the *other side* of the river. There the townspeople paid good money for the witch doctor's medicine; a local grocer even shelved some. The sisters were treated respectfully. They weren't teased for being the granddaughters of a Voodoo priestess. People addressed them and sought their opinions. There was also a lot of attention from men, especially towards Mags.

Mags carried her petite and curvy body on an upbeat rhythm that only she could hear. Lotti, however, kept her mind on the money and her petite yet sturdy frame planted firmly on the ground.

The Auguste girls were nine months apart in age. People used to mistake them for twins. Lotti, being the eldest, was serious-minded, while Mags acquired all the personality. She shined like a diamond amongst coal. Her dresses, although the same as Lotti's, always fit a little shorter and tighter. All the men noticed her striking figure.

14

It was Mags' body that stopped them from selling potions from door-to-door and kept them walking swiftly through the woods, over the bridge, and into town to sell them where there was safety in numbers. Even there, young men whispered sweet nothings in Mags' ears, while older men promised her money and fancy gifts.

However, it was a particularly young, slick-haired mulatto brother from up north who eventually tore the business and the duo apart.

BLACK VELVET

Richard W. Owens wafted into town on a northern wind, hauling trouble and toxic pleasures. He was a saxophone player for a popular big band that toured throughout Baton Rouge and New Orleans.

It was a typical hot and hazy mid-summer afternoon in town where Lotti and Mags sold their potions when Richard came visiting with a friend between gigs. The men were moving on from a late breakfast at a frequented brothel in Davidsonville. While aimlessly driving along a tatty road, they caught sight of Lotti and Mags. Unaware of being watched, the sisters were giggling, bumping, and teasing one another as they walked.

"Slow down, brother, slow down," Richard insisted, nudging his friend. "Do you see what I see? Hmph, have mercy!"

"Ah sho do. Ah sho do," his friend responded slyly, slowing down. "Now let's see if dey front matches dey back."

Lotti and Mags were heading up the road to Mrs. Lemelle's house; her ailing husband, Abe, required a gout potion. Suddenly, a sleek black, well-polished 1946 *Cadillac* convertible coupe rolled slowly beside them.

Richard leaned through the window and brushed his hand gently into Mags. His friend stopped the car.

"I've seen plenty of dolls throughout my days, but never any as beautiful as black velvet," Richard crooned in a deep, soothing, northern slang. Mags stopped dead in her tracks. He gently kissed her hand. "Delighted to make your acquaintance, Miss...?"

"What's dat, mista? Black what? We ain't want none." Lotti jumped in front of Mags and pulled her away. "Come on, we gotta go! Pa will send out an army if we ain't home soon," she lied, yelling behind them.

Mags stopped, pulled away from her sister's grasp, and walked back to the car. She extended her hands to Richard, and he gathered them into his own.

"Miss Mary Magdalene Auguste, sir," she whispered slowly and invitingly, gazing into Richard's eyes. "Dis here is my sistah, Miss Charlotte Auguste," she nodded toward Lotti. "Folks 'round here call her Lotti, me Mags. You can call me Mary."

Lotti froze in disbelief. Mags had transformed from a free spirit into a temptress in the blink of an eye. She seemed taller; her eyes sultry. With every word, the arch in her back deepened. A sly smile crept along one side of her face and with every breath, her bosom grew. Mags became bait to Richard's hunger and greed.

"Richard W. Owens," the mulatto brother responded, nodding in salutations. "How do you do, Miss Mary, Miss Charlotte? May I step out, ma'am?"

"Please do," Mags purred, her words vibrating through the midday air.

"This is my old friend, Mr. Toussaint," Richard announced while stepping out of the car. "He's showing me around your lovely town.

"Howdy do, ladies. Howdy do?" Mr. Toussaint awkwardly snickered.

Richard extended his hand to Lotti. She stared at it for a second before choosing to give him a five. He smiled and respectfully nodded his head. Her heart skipped a beat at the glimpse of his sparkling eyes and deep dimples.

17

"Ladies, I'm playing tonight at T-Rays. I would love to be accompanied by dames as beautiful as you." Richard moved closer toward Mags and rubbed a finger across her cheek. "Soft like velvet too," he added, winking his eye.

Mags deeply exhaled and sang, "We'd love to."

"Ahhh, mista—" Lotti began to interject.

"Please, don't say no. It's not every day a fella entertains angels," Richard pleaded.

He cupped Lotti's cheek and she inhaled the enticing aroma of his mildly woodsy cologne. It strayed from his tailored chest and tickled her nose. His breath smelled of the peppermint candy he rolled in his mouth.

Lotti tilted her head and confined his hand between her cheek and shoulder. "What time did you say?"

What time did you say often replayed in Lotti's mind. Her muttered question to the *black velvet fella* swirled in outer space, then turned and smacked her in the head. She wished she'd never asked. *What time did you say* stole precious moments no longer shared between sisters, while days turned into years without each other. *What time did you say* ungraciously removed the carelessness of their youthful years. Their days of skipping rocks, running aimlessly through meadows, and purposely lying in the sun were taken. *What time did you say* eventually stole the contentedness of Lotti's solitary existence and left her remorseful and pregnant with Richard's baby. She swore she'd never ask *what time did you say* again. She'd make her own time and seize her own moments.

J.C. MILLER

BLACK VELVET TRAVESTY

Lotti was twenty years old and four months pregnant when her grandmother was murdered. She was lynched; beaten and hung from an old oak tree. Her body was discovered a few feet away from the tree wrapped in burlap as if to be carried away to another location. The remains of a soot-covered wooden cross accompanied her like a blazing symbol of the assailant's faith.

The girls, secretly caught in the whirlwind of what Lotti had labeled the *Black Velvet Travesty*, were supposedly out with a girlfriend that evening. The truth was they danced into the wee hours of the morning listening to Richard's band. When they arrived home, the police and fire department were there. Their shack had burnt to the ground. The authorities explained that their closest neighbors reported smoke and assured the sisters that *no bodies were found* before proceeding to question their whereabouts. No one knew where The Grandmother may have gone; her body was found later that evening forty miles out from their small town.

Lotti and Mags waited until daybreak to visit the site. The body had been removed, and the area was taped off. The girls stood clinging to one another as they attempted to piece the mystery together. Ten minutes into their mourning, they noticed an older black man nearby. He was gazing at the oak tree but didn't make a sound.

"Can we help you?" Lotti asked, pushing Mags behind her.

He turned and stated, "Ah seen what done happened to ya maw-maw."

19

He went on to tell them about a parked pickup truck and the three men in white sheets he saw there; he even overheard their names. They were in the process of moving The Grandmother's body when he stepped on a branch, alerting them to his presence. They chased him but the older man, familiar with the area where he hunted bullfrogs, lost them, hiding in an abandoned, camouflaged duck blind.

"Dey searched for me for near about an hour. Ah sat o'va in dat blind praying and de Lord heard me. A police car drove by. Dey spoke. Den er'rybody went der separate ways. Ah waited a while longer den hot-footed back home. Ah wasn't fixin' to call de police, den ah figured ya maw-maw done been through enough. So, ah called but ah ain't say who ah was tho. No, ma'am."

"Dey never mentioned any calls," Mags stated, suspiciously.

"Ah reckon not. Dey all get along real friendly lak round here."

Lotti and Mags knew who the men in white sheets were and gathered not much would be done.

"Ah guess ah should be leaving town soon. Don't want no trouble," the older man stated.

"No need, Mistah. Ah wouldn't worry if ah was you. Give it tree days. Ah guarantee you ain't got no worries, dey do!" The Grandmother declared, her spirit speaking through Lotti.

Over the next three days, each murderer was found dead.

On the first day, Klan leader and local pastor that had harassed The Grandmother in the past, Reverend White, or *Sweaty Pig,* as The Grandmother called him, was found dead in his home. He choked to death on a bone while eating supper. Deacon Breaux, the reverend's flunky, ran his car off of the road on day two. He hit a tree and died upon impact. On night three, Walter Hebert, an ex-con who was known to like his liquor and women, was called in dead by a prostitute; heart attack.

LOVE SPELL

Hardly anything was salvageable from the small shack in the bayou. The Grandmother's boiling pot and Lotti's metal lock box containing her revival Bible, all of her earnings, and a picture of she, Mags, and Richard at T-Rays were the only items saved.

The sisters left Baton Rouge and never looked back. They continued to compete for the love of the traveling sax-man who only loved himself. In the end, they grew distant and never regained their childhood friendship.

Mags followed Richard to New Orleans and traveled as a showgirl with his band. Her years of practicing captivating attention prepared her for the spotlight. She quickly gained recognition and starred in a few shows. *Miss Mary Mags,* as she was known, swung her hips, whined her waist, and teased her way into the hearts of longing men and the envy of women. She and Richard continued to accompany one another. He introduced her to a world different from the one she knew, and she instantly became its lover. Her charming ways allotted her possession of all she desired, except him. Mags loved Richard, but Richard loved all women. Eventually, she grew tired of his unfaithfulness and reached out to Lotti, who was doing domestic work in Gonzales, Louisiana, for help.

Lotti found unexpected pleasure assisting her sister because the two hadn't spoken in years. Getting straight to business, they danced, chanted, and worshipped; calling on the spirits of the ancestors to *ride* (enter) them under a possession. After many days, one of The

Grandmother's roots was concocted to capture Richard's heart and turn him back to Mags. The remainder of Mags' visit with Lotti was short, polite, and centered around the beautiful caramel-colored five-year-old that Lotti shared with the man Mags loved. Mags welcomed Puah Marie Auguste into her life, but the sisters never discussed her being Richard's daughter.

The spell didn't keep Richard's eyes from roaming, but his heart was now under lock and key. He and Mags married, but they never conceived children. They moved to New York City where they owned and operated a blues club and a bar, amongst a few unsavory business affairs.

TIME SLIPPED AWAY

"No man should come 'tween relation, especially one too smooth to hold on to," Lotti would often say. "Never loves a man dat's prettier den you. Never loves a man dat can't love ya lak him loves himself," she expressed on her *sad* days.

Sad days when she listened to *sad* music and dawdled about in her *sad*-looking muumuu. She sipped on *sad* moonshine that she made in a tub of *sad* tears. Lotti wasn't so much sad about Richard, but sad because of what she lost while waiting for him:*time.*

Time slipped away from Lotti while she hid behind the shadows of darkness in her home where the cypress trees hang low, and the swamp air smelled of lavender and rosemary. She hid back in the bayou where dirt roads end and clay paths began; that's where she boiled sheets and raised an altogether perfect granddaughter named Rahab.

J.C. MILLER

PUAH

SILVER SPOON

Born Friday, April 11, 1952, in the servant's quarters of the Fontaine plantation a far from modest two-story Antebellum French Colonial mansion in Gonzales, Louisiana. You can say Puah was *born with a silver spoon in her mouth*

The Fontaine plantation, one of the largest sugarcane producers in Louisiana, was highly lucrative in its heyday. It had been shut down over a decade before Puah Marie Auguste graced its halls.

When Lotti first met them, Dr. Fontaine was running for office. Mrs. Fontaine, blueblood herself, was settling well into her position as wife, mother, and head over numerous charity boards. The Missus, during one of her visits into town, literally stumbled over Lotti who had fainted directly in front of her. Mrs. Fontaine immediately administered care. She knelt beside Lotti, fanning her with a dainty lace hand-fan. When Lotti came to, she mistook her for an angel. Mrs. Fontaine was a rather lovely woman. She was pale in complexion. A few freckles danced across the bridge of her nose. Her hair, thick and bouncy, laid on her shoulders in red curls and her eyes played tricks with hues of green. Lotti couldn't help but stare. She looked like a porcelain doll.

"Are you okay?" Mrs. Fontaine asked repeatedly.

"Yes'm, I'm fine."

"Would you like a ride home?"

"No'm, I'm just a few blocks down at de Red Light Motel," Lotti answered, managing to sit up.

A small curious crowd gathered in front of them.

"Nonsense. You're not well. Poor thing, I'll take you there," Mrs. Fontaine insisted, helping Lotti to her feet.

The crowd dispersed.

"No, ma'am, I'm not sick...just a little pregnant, and a lot hungry. Missed breakfast dis morning rushing to sell my potions to de grocer before he opened. Ah probably done missed lunch by now," Lotti admitted, noticing a few broken bottles of her antidotes swept over to the curb. "Thank you, ma'am, for helping."

"You know I was just about to have a late lunch? Done ran myself silly today. Please join me...or I'm liable to faint myself."

The two women dined al fresco at a French café and discussed their situations. The Fontaine's live-in nanny unexpectedly eloped and moved out of state leaving Mrs. Fontaine with the predicament of interviewing for a replacement in addition to her other daily loyalties. Lotti, needing a steady job and home for her new arrival, took advantage of the situation. She passionately expressed her suitability for the job although she had no prior experience. She was a fast-talker and could swindle her way into anything. Lotti played the sympathy card. She spoke of The Grandmother's recent passing and how Mags ran off with her baby's father. Mrs. Fontaine felt deep compassion and offered Lotti the position. Before the day's end, Lotti was moved into the Fontaine home and largest room in the servant's quarters. It had an adjoining bathroom that was bigger than any home she, Mags, or The Grandmother had ever lived in. Mrs. Fontaine also allowed her to use a small room upstairs near the nurseries while the children were still young. Lotti had no oppositions. She only required a day off to sell her potions and boil sheets.

The stair-step Fontaine trio were lovingly and sternly cared for by Lotti for nearly twenty years. She nursed them, groomed them, fed them, defended them, and made sure each child felt as much love as she gave Puah. The Fontaine's were more than employers; they were extended family. They treated Puah like their own. She ate her meals at the table with them, took music lessons with the girls, holidayed with the family, and attended formal events. Puah grew in beauty, charm, and grace. She was spoiled by her Aunt Mags and sheltered by the comforts of a lavish home. It was no wonder she would fall.

YOUNG LOVE

During the annual Gonzales, Louisiana *Jambalaya Festival*, Puah fell from grace. She had recently graduated from high school and was awaiting nursing school in the Fall. Puah was also very much in love with the youngest Fontaine child, Daphne.

Puah and Daphne rode every ride at the festival at least twice. They played games, shared cola, fries, and cotton candy. They skipped through the park holding hands, giggling, and whispering secrets. No one mattered. They'd soon be separated again. Puah would be attending a local nursing school while Daphne was to start her second year at *Harvard.* There wasn't time to care about the world around them; only their love mattered.

As night fell, the festival attendees gathered in the parking lot to watch the fireworks. Puah and Daphne separated themselves from the crowd and snuck away to the bleachers. Hiding, they watched the fireworks, made plans, and enjoyed each other's attention.

Puah and Daphne weren't always in love. Love happened along the way. They spent most of their childhood arguing with one another. Everyone charged it off as being the youngest child and only child syndrome. Daphne was never the girlish type; she'd rather play baseball than attend the many socials required of her. She detested the fancy cotillions and loathed the gawking boys. She felt awkward in beauty compared to her charming siblings. Her mother often compared her to herself as a child, an odd duckling awaiting to become a swan. Daphne

29

saw no future swan through her clumsy demeanor, red hair, freckled face, and lanky stature.

Puah, on the other hand, was already enchanting. She was leggy and slender in stature, perfect for the cover of any magazine. Her soft, curly, black hair framed her caramel colored round face in a short bob. She was the romantic dreamer only allowed to attend *the ball* as a server. She couldn't participate, it wasn't her place. She sat along the floral textile walls sipping punch and longing to be a debutante in a *coming-out* event. Puah couldn't understand why Daphne used her as a decoy when she could be dancing the night away. Instead, they giggled and laughed at the debutantes and their forward attempts to entice young escorts. Puah needed no scheming enticements. The young men were already sneaking glances of her while dancing with the dignified debs. When retrieving drinks for the thirsty young ladies in waiting, the escorts often smiled or winked at Puah. Some even dared to say hi. After a while, Puah wasn't allowed to attend anymore. She was stealing attention meant for blue blood.

It was the night of Daphne's high school prom that she and Puah discovered new feelings toward one another. Daphne arrived home early that evening crying. Her date practically tossed her out of his car and sped off. Puah was sitting on the front porch listening to records, learning new dances, and drinking pop with a suitor, Minton Silas Williams, Jr. He was a bright and handsome young man. Newly graduated from college, Minton was an eligible bachelor with schoolboy charm. His parents were owner-operators of a local dry cleaning business. They had intentions to open a second location in New Orleans for

Minton to run. Lotti admired his possibilities, and Mrs. Fontaine approved of her choice. The two women arranged his and Puah's courtship with a little bribery on Mrs. Fontaine's part. Minton's father wasn't a fan of Lotti's Voodoo background but agreed to the courtship after learning of Puah's dowry.

As Daphne approached the porch, she noticed Puah and Minton laughing and enjoying their evening. She stood on the walkway and watched, unknown to them, as they playfully teased one another while dancing. Feeling Daphne's stare on the back of her head, Puah quickly turned and caught her gazing at them.

"You're home early," she stated, pulling herself from Minton's arms and nervously fixing her hair. "What? Charles couldn't keep up with that fancy two-step I taught you?"

Embarrassed, Daphne excused herself, crying and running around to the back of the house. Puah attempted to make a quick apology to Minton, asking him to leave, but he sighed heavily in disagreement.

He had big plans for the non-chaperoned evening. It was expected of him to ask Puah for her hand in marriage after she graduated, and they hadn't even kissed.

"I'm sorry but my sis...I mean Daphne needs me. Couldn't you tell she was crying?"

"That's the problem," Minton insisted, grabbing Puah's arms. "These people aren't your family, Pu."

Insulted, Puah tugged away. She quickly stopped the record playing on the antique Victrola causing *Jerry Butler* singing, "Never Give You Up" to come to a screeching halt then sashayed toward the steps.

31

"I believe it's time for you to leave, Mr. Williams. You shouldn't overstay your welcome," she said, stern-faced and dignified, gesturing toward the road.

Minton stared at her in disbelief. *Some things never change.* He shook his head, remembering their childhood. He tucked his hands into the pockets of his jeans, lowered his head, and shuffled his feet to the stairs where she stood.

"You may call on me Sunday after dinner," Puah added, extending her hand for him to kiss. She didn't want to lose her only companionship. The Fontaine kids were all venturing off into their own lives.

Minton stepped down onto the steps, with one foot still on the porch. He bowed his head and took Puah's hand into his. Gazing into her deeply set eyes, he pressed his lips against her hand then slowly licked up her arm. Puah's mouth fell open in repugnance and liking. She clutched her chest with her free hand, remembering the boy who used to pull her pigtails.

Only Minton Silas Williams would lick an entire arm.

"I'll most likely be busy on Sunday, Miss Auguste. But you have yourself a lovely life," he informed her, running his finger down her cheek then using it to close her mouth. "Good night," he added, before pouncing backward off the steps. He turned and walked swiftly down the walkway, proud of himself. Puah stared as he disappeared behind the trees.

"Good night," she whispered. *Please come back.*

Puah found Daphne at the gazebo crying, her face tucked into her hands.

32

"You okay, Daph?" she asked, sitting beside her and rubbing her back. The pink satin dress that she wore to the prom was wet from perspiration.

"Boys are jerks," Daphne answered, rebuking the male species.

"What happened?" Puah questioned, lifting Daphne's chin and examining her red freckled face.

"What always happens? Typical horny high school boy stuff. After he picked me up, we drove directly to Make-Out Point. He didn't even take me to my prom." She cried louder, dropping her face back into her hands. "I didn't even get to dance in this beautiful gown Tante Mags had made for me," Daphne added, fluffing out the dress. "Not that I wanted to, but I should've had the opportunity."

"Real jerk," Puah agreed.

They sat for a while in silence, allowing hurt pride to have its moment.

Then, Puah jumped to her feet and stood in front of Daphne.

"Bon jour, Miss Daphne." Puah stated, extending her hand. "Mon chéri, de evening is full of beautiful music. Please dance with me under de stars," she insisted, holding out her hand and mimicking a French accent.

Daphne stood and curtsied. Puah then took her hand, and they walked down the gazebo steps into the neatly manicured lawn. Noticing she towered over Puah's head, Daphne kicked off her shoes. They both giggled and danced around the gazebo humming Tchaikovsky's "Sleeping Beauty Waltz" very badly. The girls danced until they felt dizzy. Laughing, they collapsed on top of each other. Daphne stared into Puah's dark brown eyes and

33

brushed her curly black hair out of her face. They felt awkward.

"Pu, do you know why guys never get to first base with me."

"Why?" Puah asked curiously, knowing Judith Fontaine let her prom date, weird Daniel Hervey, get to third base. She came home that night bragging about becoming a woman in his car.

"Well, mostly because I don't like boys too much...well...I don't like them much at all." Daphne ran a finger around Puah's cheek. "I would much rather feel the soft touch of a woman," she proclaimed, kissing Puah uninvited and unexpectedly. Puah kissed her back.

They spent that night together not arguing or fighting as spoiled kids do but sharing secrets and curiosities as women.

DEGRADING A DEBUTANTE

The girls were hiding under the bleachers enthralled by the pleasures of puppy love when Daphne's brother, John Jr., loudly called their names.

"Daphne, Pu!" he yelled, in confusion and disbelief. The equally astonished young blonde-haired girl who was with him yelped and covered her mouth.

"What the heck are you doing?" John Jr. questioned, pulling his sister from Puah's embrace. His face flushed with anger. His icy blue eyes spoke of the hatred his words couldn't describe.

"Tee-John, I...we..." Daphne attempted to explain, but sudden embarrassment left her speechless.

"Go to father's car right now," he insisted, pointing toward the parking lot.

"But we came with Mama—"

"Go! I'll handle Lotti," John Jr. shouted, interrupting and sternly gesturing her away.

He turned to his blonde-haired date and whispered something in her ear before kissing her cheek. She coyly smiled and walked away satisfied.

"Pu...Puah. I can't tell you how disappointed I am in you," John Jr. said in a condescending tone. His sifting eyes perched upon Puah's soul. "Wait here," he added, exiting from under the bleachers.

Puah's stomach dropped.

John Jr. was the only Fontaine to ever display poor mannerism toward her. She knew he would tell. She knew he had grown embarrassed by his family's involvement with her and her Voodoo loving mother. John Jr. smoked a cigarette then left to find Lotti, gesturing to Puah to stay put. She sat under the bleachers for twenty minutes trying to put together a plan for her and Daphne to run away.

"If you run, so help me I'll tell," John Jr. threatened when he came back.

He grabbed Puah by the arm and pulled her out to his silver 1969 Ford Mustang, then tossed her in and slammed the door. He sped down the empty highway, passing the plantation. Puah was afraid to speak. She didn't like the cold gaze in his eyes nor the tightening of his chiseled cheekbones. He finally pulled over by a lake in the bayou, then got out of the car to smoke another cigarette.

Why did I get in this car? It would've been better to take the backlash. No telling what he's got planned for me. A black girl, degrading the name of a debutante in the south. No telling.

When John Jr. finished his smoke, he flicked the butt into the lake and nonchalantly walked back to the car. He forcefully pulled Puah out by her hair. She screamed, pressing his hand down on her head to keep him from ripping the hair from her scalp. He threw her to the ground and straddled her. Puah slapped him so hard that it drew blood from his lip. He licked the wound and slapped her back. They proceeded to wrestle. Uninvited and unexpectedly, John Jr. kissed her, but she didn't kiss him back. She fought. When he grew tired of fighting, he raped her.

DAY BREAK

John Jr. left Puah by the lake to fend for herself. She lay stiff on the ground in the dark and waited to die. She wanted the earth to seep her into a sinkhole.

Being underground would be better than living out this misery.

When Puah finally accepted that the earth would not swallow her and she had no more tears to cry, she picked herself up disheartened but not vanquished. Death's denial recharged her. She walked seven miles back to the plantation fueled on repugnance.

Masked by the dry mud covering her body and dress, Puah mimicked Lotti's chanting and called on the spirits until she felt a surge of energy rush through her body. As anger and rage set in, she began to feel stronger. She would have Lotti curse John Jr.'s manhood so that he'd never be able to have relations again.

Puah quietly entered the house near daybreak. She tipped into Daphne's room prepared to rescue her. She was convinced they could run away and start a new life together. The room was dim with the colors of sunrise peeking through lace curtains.

John Jr.'s silhouette curved over Daphne. Their moans competed with the deep beating of Puah's heart. Puah stood in the corner and watched as every dream she's ever had shattered. She wanted to believe he was raping his sister as he had raped her. She wanted to believe Daphne was fighting back, but they kissed. Puah's mouth pooled with saliva. She stepped out from the darkened corner and regurgitated onto the defiled bed. Daphne screamed.

"Pu! Let's talk about this," John Jr. insisted, lunging toward her.

Puah escaped his attempts. She ran out of the bedroom and down the hall as fast as she could. She held her mouth and didn't make a sound. Doors popped open, lights turned on, and voices questioned, but Puah never stopped. She continued to run from the Fontaine plantation, with no plans of ever returning.

John Jr. convinced his parents that he came into Daphne's room after hearing strange noises. He explained that he discovered she and Puah in bed together. He said that Daphne screamed when she noticed him.

"That's a lie," Daphne rebuked, hysterically crying.

John Jr. continued the fabrication, stating he tried to contain Puah, but she escaped, and that Daphne threw up because she was overcome with fear. He also added that he and the blonde-haired girl caught them earlier at the field. He thought that after a stern talking to the matter had blown over.

Mrs. Fontaine, feeling sick herself, was enraged. She searched for clarification from her trembling daughter, obviously naked under the soiled sheets she held underneath her chin. Finding no explanation, she swiftly exited the room yelling, "Lotti!"

Hearing the initial scream, Lotti threw on a housecoat and ran out of her room. She was already at the bottom of the stairs waiting with the other servants when Mrs. Fontaine rushed down hurling insults and accusations toward her. The Missus insisted that Daphne, who was crying behind her, declaring her love for Puah, would have nothing to do with such degraded behavior. Lotti stood firm and still. She held her peace out of respect. She knew the dream was nearing an end. They'd been under the Fontaine's roof for far too long. No one needed a nanny any longer. She was now the *help*.

Her mind wandered toward her daughter's safety as Mrs. Fontaine's rant continued. Dr. Fontaine attempted to calm her, but she raged like a storm with unleashed fury. Lotti was ordered to leave that day, at that moment, with everything they owned.

Lotti made several trips from the house to a motel until she gathered all of their belongings. It was the same motel she lived nineteen years ago. It was also she and Puah's place of refuge.

"If any'ting ever goes wrong, I'll meet ya here," Lotti instructed, drilling it in Puah's head from a child. "Der's no telling with white folk. Best be safe den sorry."

On Lotti's last trip back to the plantation, she handed Mrs. Fontaine her car keys. Mrs. Fontaine, who was still wearing a pink silk housecoat and satin hair bonnet, cried inconsolably. She knew she had lost her best friend. She rocked in her favorite rocking chair on the front porch, sipping on her fifth *Bloody Mary*.

"Never come back here again, Charlotte Auguste. You stole from me. I gave you everything, and you stole from me," she managed to mutter.

"Yes'm," Lotti solemnly responded, nodding. If my baby's hurt, I'll be back to tear this sucker down and everyone in it. I guarantee.

FIDDLING WITH FATE

Late that night, Puah made her way to the motel.

Falling into Lotti's arms, Puah told everything that happened. Not blinking an eye or skipping a beat, Lotti quietly assisted her daughter. She pulled out some dried herbs and made a special tea for her to sip on while she drew a hot tub of water. Lotti washed Puah with hyssop and lavender castile soap, then rubbed her down in warm healing oils. Before putting Puah to bed, Lotti fluffed the pillows on the dreary looking mattress and smoothed the sheets with her pressing hands. She waited until Puah fell asleep before slipping out of the room with vengeance in her heart. Had Lotti known all that took place, she would've slapped Mrs. Fontaine. Had she known she would've given John Jr. the skinning he rightly deserved. Instead, Lotti hitched a ride to Baton Rouge to settle the score the only way she knew how; through black magic. She didn't discuss what she did, all that mattered was Puah's wishes were honored, and John Jr. would never enjoy the pleasures of relations again.

After returning from Baton Rouge, Lotti attempted to sleep but could find no rest. Her mind raced, still charged with black magic. Twice she'd allowed her feelings to overshadow wisdom and called on the Voodoo queen. Her emotions ran a bill her heart couldn't pay; dark magic thrives on death, the selling of souls. Lotti was a soul behind in payment. The queen avenged The Grandmother's murder as a favor, but she warned Lotti if she ever returned, she'd owe her. Lotti tossed and turned on the lumpy mattress. The darkened motel room felt

40

damp and smelled of mildew. She couldn't spray the permeating odor away, so she burnt candles to mask it. Seeking tranquility, she drank a cup of herbal tea with a shot of corn liquor. The concoctions effects soothed her, but a broken sign hanging above their room door zapped every five minutes and kept her from sleeping soundly. She decided she shouldn't sleep. There was too much to do. She struggled up from the bumpy bed, missing the comfort of the one she formerly used and anxiously began reorganizing their belongings.

Lotti could hardly wait for Minton to arrive. He was the only person she knew to call other than Mags, who lived too far. Minton Williams, Puah's former suitor, put an end to Puah *stringing him along* some time ago. In spite of he and Puah's differences, Lotti acquainted him with everything that happened then asked for help in moving them to New Orleans. Minton hesitated at first. He started not to come, but Lotti persuasively reminded him of what a lovely couple he and Puah once made. She insisted that *"destiny is at work and you shouldn't fiddle with fate."* Minton didn't give a direct time to expect him. He merely noted he'd be there. After the *Fontaine Fiasco,* they could all use a fresh start.

LEAVING GONZALES

It was high noon when Minton showed up at the door of the foul-smelling motel room. Lotti was pleased to see a familiar smiling face. He was taller than she recalled. His boyish charm gave way to a well sculptured, milk chocolate covered, ruggedly handsome young man.

Wearing a painted smile across her solemn face, Puah softly spoke as though rehearsed, "Hello Minton. It's good to see you. Thank you kindly for helping us." Her glazed over eyes told the real story.

Minton didn't know if he should kiss her cheek or shake her hand. He settled on, "Hello."

Puah slightly tilted her head in approval, like a proper debutante, before bursting into tears and running into the bathroom.

"Don't mind her none; she's got a lot of healing to do. It's so good to see ya," Lotti stated, changing the topic. She handed Minton two suitcases before he could respond.

"It's good to see you too, Mama Lotti," he halfheartedly agreed, taking the bags and walking out of the door.

"It's all gonna be alright, you'll see," Lotti added, loudly enough for them both to hear.

Minton packed their things into his new cherry red *Ford F100* pickup. Puah cried in the bathroom the entire time. When the packing was complete, he had to physically pick her up and carry her out to the vehicle. His heart raced with anger imagining the over-privileged, ivy-league schooled Fontaine boy raping his girl. He sat at the wheel hot with a hatred he'd never felt before. He

42

contemplated heading to the plantation. Afraid of himself and the love he felt for Puah; his hands tightly gripped the steering wheel. *Could I possibly kill someone?*

"Just drive, Minton. You'd be arrested fuh' sho. Don't worry none, Mama Lotti done handled it," Lotti affirmed, smiling. She reached over Puah's lap and patted him on his thigh. "Ain't no use," she stated louder, freeing him of any plots.

Minton beat the steering wheel with his fist a few times before tossing his arm around Puah's shoulders and pulling her close. He drove off, leaving Gonzales behind. Puah felt the warmth of familiarity and the safety of strength in his arms. She snuggled close to him and fell asleep.

NO RETURN ADDRESS

After leaving Gonzales, Puah stopped speaking altogether and barely ate anything. Minton lost patience with her quickly. He welcomed the women to use the bedroom of his bachelor pad in Faubourg Tremé outside of the French Quarter. He slept on the couch behind a mountain of their belongings.

He bought Puah flowers, massaged her feet, tried his hand at feeding her, and attempted to engage her in conversation, but it was in vain. All she did was cry.

The more flowers Minton bought for Puah the more women frequented his dry cleaning business. There had never been such an outburst of stained blouses in New Orleans. Lotti watched from a distance as she helped with his business, adding her secret scent to his wash. He was doing well for himself, and it was a good thing because he spent entirely too much money. He bought all new state of the art machinery, fancy clothes, and blew tons of cash entertaining misery away.

One night, Minton came home drunk and made a forward advance toward Puah. She slapped him, and Lotti gathered it was time for them to go.

"She needs time. Space to heal." She tried to explain to Minton's deaf ears, but women were practically dropping their undergarments at his feet, and Puah's nonsense was wearing thin.

Lotti made Minton her famous seafood gumbo before moving back into the bayou where she could boil sheets, make potions, detour babies, and nurse Puah back to health. She prepared him a bowl of gumbo over rice, piled high with shrimp and a few drops of Puah's menstrual blood to affirm his devotion while she recuperated.

In the following months, Puah's health continued to decline, and she refused to speak. Lotti was nearing the end of her wits. She knew the powers of darkness were against her, but that motivated her to fight harder. There were nights she considered heading back to Gonzales to kill John Jr. with her bare hands. She resisted, finding comfort in the spell cast on him. *A life of torture would suit him better than death.* She decided to settle her dealings with Mrs. Fontaine instead. Lotti sat down and wrote a long letter describing how the Fontaine's *perfect* house and *perfect* family were a *perfect mess.* She revealed their secrets and addressed what happened between Puah, Daphne, and John Jr. that night. Lotti mailed the letter with no fear, guilt, doubt, or return address.

TO GOD IN PRAYER

Puah fainted one morning while getting in the shower and had to be rushed to the hospital. That same morning, A young pastor stopped by the hospital to pray with a terminally ill parishioner from his church, The House of Judah. Before leaving, he routinely walked through the emergency area praying for the sick. When Pastor Josh met Lotti, she was coming through the sliding doors struggling to assist Puah. He immediately offered his help. Lotti hesitated at first, noticing he was a *man of the cloth* but needing help she agreed. Pastor Josh sat with Puah while Lotti filled out hospital forms. Puah was trembling, so he placed his Bible and hat down on the seat next to them and took her cold skeletal hands into his. Her beautiful face was thin and beaten with sadness. *Be with her, Lord. Help Your child.* He prayed before closing his eyes for a moment to reflect on his busy day. He hummed, then sang a soothing hymn while warming Puah's cold hands.

"O what peace we often forfeit, O what needless pain we bear, All because we do not carry, Everything to God in prayer."

Pastor Josh sang tenderly. Opening his eyes, he gently directed Puah's attention toward him. "God sees all, and He already knows, beb. He knows all about your troubles. *For ah know de thoughts dat ah think toward you...thoughts of peace, and not of evil, to give you hope and a future.* It's gonna be alright," he assured.

Puah looked into the eyes of the placid young pastor. He looked no more than ten years her senior. *What*

46

does he know? She rolled her eyes and leaned her throbbing head on his broad shoulder.

"Take it to de Lord in prayer. It's okay to let go and live again. Leave your pain in de past. *He heals de broken in heart and binds up der wounds.* You will have peace again; you will have joy again."

She relaxed her shoulders as Pastor Josh's words played like an encouraging song in the back of her mind.

"You...will...have a beautiful, healthy baby girl and life will go on," Pastor Josh prophesied, slowly pondering over every revealed word.

Puah was startled upright. She slowly turned her pounding head toward him in full attention. *How did he know?* Her eyes filled with tears.

"Jesus knows our every weakness. Take it to de Lord in prayer," he continued to sing, more enthusiastically.

Puah groaned and rocked to and fro as if fighting the devil himself for the return of her voice. She finally yelped. "Oooh! Help me; I don't wanna die. I just can't live. I don't want to. Please, help me..."

Lotti threw the tedious paperwork she was filling out back at the agitated nurse and ran to Puah's side.

"Pu! Beb, you alright?" Lotti fussed over her, checking her forehead, neck, and cheeks for fever.

"Yes, Mama," Puah cried, taking her mother's busy hands into hers to kiss. She felt like she was waking up from a nightmare. Days had turned into nights, weeks into months, and they all seemed like one long horrible dream. Puah had attempted to will her life away. She desperately tried to ignore what was happening in and around her. "I'm pregnant, Mama," she admitted, coming to herself.

"No, Pu, you not. You don seen ya menstrual a few times naw, ah knows," Lotti interrupted, getting down on her knees. They were buckling under her.

"I'm not asking, Mama, I'm telling you. I'm pregnant. I've felt kicking and fluttering for a while. I saw a whole foot press against my belly the other day. I just didn't care. I don't know how to explain it. I feel dead, but I'm not."

Everyone in the emergency waiting area stared, engaged in the saga unfolding in front of them.

"I don't care about anything anymore. I feel like...like I don't want to live. I don't want his baby; I hate him, Mama," Puah cried, leaning over her mother who was crying in her lap.

Lotti cried because she knew the curse was beginning. She knew she hadn't fulfilled her end of the bargain. All she needed was more time to figure things out. *"Ya baby's baby will be cursed, and she will carry ya weight upon her shoulders. Until ah get my sacrifice, ya burdens she will carry."* Lotti shivered, hearing the dark Voodoo queen's threatening words echo through her mind.

LAVENDER FIELD

After several failed attempts to naturally abort the baby without harming Puah, Lotti surrendered. Puah was too far along and too weak to attempt an actual abortion. Lotti's old tricks of chewing on cinnamon sticks, Chamomile sitz baths, and vaginally inserting fresh parsley sprigs failed her.

"She's latched good," Lotti proclaimed, feeling defeated.

"Do whatever it takes, Mama."

"Pu! Tink about your future. Don't you want other childr'n? We gonna figure dis thang out once she's here."

"Will you kill her?"

Puah didn't want John Jr.'s baby, and Lotti couldn't fault her for that, but she had become desperate, and that worried Lotti. The two spoke of giving the baby up for adoption, but Lotti knew that wouldn't reverse the curse. *Death was better than being born into a doomed existence.*

A few weeks later, the day after Lotti dreamt of a fragrant field covered in lavender bushes for miles and miles, Rahab Auguste was born. Both women agreed that she was the smallest baby they'd ever seen, but she breathed well on her own and had ten little fingers and toes. She looked like a runt, yet she had as much spunk and determination as the *pick of the litter.* Lotti named her Rahab, *meaning fierce and spacious.* She was bright, demanding attention just like the field in Lotti's dream. Rahab was chosen to live, and Lotti instantly fell in love. *No left-handed Voodoo will mess with either of my girls.*

49

Lotti was the granddaughter of a Voodoo priestess, and she would die protecting her family.

As the days progressed into months, it seemed Rahab would have been better off not being born. Puah hadn't lost her desire to die, in fact, her depression grew deeper, and she was having thoughts of suicide. She shared no affections toward the baby. She hardly acknowledged her. Lotti tended to all of Rahab's needs. All Puah did was watch, cry, and imagine life without her. She didn't want to remember John Jr., but Rahab's slowly opening blueish-green colored eyes were a constant reminder, and Puah couldn't stomach her.

What kind of wretched woman am I, that I would hate my child? I'm better off dead. They'll be better off without me.

J.C. MILLER

OPPORTUNITY KNOCKS

One day, at the same time Puah was contemplating suicide, in walked Minton Williams. He was glad when the women left his apartment, but no matter how hard he tried to forget Puah he couldn't erase her memory. He had officially started dating a woman of high standing, and it was brought to his attention, by her parents, that he should ask for her hand in marriage. It seemed the right thing to do in spite of the gnawing feeling in the pit of his stomach. A feeling that kept reminding him, he and Puah belonged together.

On the eve of the family's proposal dinner, Minton sold his property to a fellow entrepreneur friend. They'd been privately discussing it for some time. As the dinner date neared so did the desire to run. That next morning, he broke his apartment lease, packed up his pickup, and rented a hotel room outside of town for the night. The prospective fiancé would be a *no-show* for the proposal dinner that evening. Minton didn't have the nerve to *call it off* with her family. Instead, he ran, but he didn't want to run alone. There was unfinished business in the bayou named Puah.

"Hello, I'm Minton Williams. I'm sorry I thought this was the Auguste residence," Minton said, introducing himself to Ms. Ruby. Ms. Ruby, Pastor Josh's mother, volunteered to keep an eye on Rahab and Puah along with her grandson, Salmone, during the day while Lotti worked.

Minton stood on the porch searching Ms. Ruby's blank face for answers. She stood behind a locked screen door with baby Salmone whining in her arms. Rahab was

51

crying in the background. "I can see you have your hands full. I'll recheck my address," he continued, not allowing her to answer.

Ms. Ruby unlocked the door and responded. "You at de right house, come on in, sugah." She sat Salmone in a high chair and gave him his lunch. She then hurried to tend to Rahab. "Ah can hardly tink straight with des two rascals carrying on all day," she laughed, keeping busy. "You a friend of Pu's?"

"Ahh, yes, ma'am, I am. We grew up together in Gonzales," Minton answered, wondering where everyone was. "Maybe this is a bad time? I'll come—"

"No, no you fine. Pu in der." Ms. Ruby nodded toward a closed door. "She should be out here tendin' to her baby tho!" Ms. Ruby shouted loud enough for Puah to hear.

"Excuse me, you said...Puah's baby?" Minton asked, confused. His heart raced. He'd been selfish in thinking Puah waited on him. The thought of her resuming life suddenly dawned on him.

"Yes, dis here is Rahab. We call her Rah, ain't she just precious?" Ms. Ruby answered, displaying the cooing baby in her arms.

"Ahh, yeah. Yes, ma'am, precious." Minton took two steps backward toward the door. Everything suddenly became defined, selling the property, breaking his lease, ditching his girl. *What have I done?* He wanted to leave.

"Wait naw, Pu's here. Ya wanna see her don't ya?" Ms. Ruby asked, walking over to the closed door and knocking before he could escape. "Ya got company, Pu. Nice lookin' fella," she yelled. "Go on in, chile. Don't mind

52

her none tho. She gon' be alright by and by," she warned, opening the door and gesturing him in.

Minton walked into the dim room. Puah was sitting on the edge of the bed with her back turned to the door staring at a drawn window. She didn't acknowledge his greetings. So, he quietly walked over. *A baby?* He then realized who the baby resembled. Peering over Puah's shoulder, he noticed a razor in her hand and her wrist turned up upon her knee.

"What you wanna do that for?" Minton asked in a deep baritone voice, startling her. He quickly grabbed both of her arms.

"Get off me," Puah demanded, struggling and dropping the blade to the ground.

"Run away with me," Minton blurted before he could change his mind. He hunched over her with his arms wrapped around her waist. He kissed the side of her neck. She smelled of lavender and sweet rosemary. He wanted to kiss her again but decided not to press his luck. She hadn't smacked him yet. "I can't stop thinking about you, Pu. Let's leave this God forsaken state together," he continued softly so Ms. Ruby couldn't hear his pleading.

Puah sobbed, embracing his strong arms around her waist. She started to pull them away, but she felt safe. She allowed her body to relax against his. Puah wanted someone to rescue her. She needed a life do-over, or she would die.

"I sold my business, and I'm moving to New York in the morning."

Puah's body stiffened. Minton had her full attention. "I feel like I can't breathe here anymore. I need to start over." He spoke her mind. "Problem is, I can't leave without you, beb," he revealed, sitting down and scooping her into his arms.

Puah was thin but healthy looking. She no longer wore the cute bob haircut. Her hair grew out and hung down her back in a thick, curly ponytail. Puah wrapped her arms around Minton's neck and tucked her head on his shoulder. She knew she had to tell him about Rahab.

"I have a baby now," she stated softly, staring him in his eyes. She wanted to witness his face grimace in disgust. "I hate her, she's Tee-John's baby," Puah continued, noticing no discontentment in him. She closed her eyes feeling sick to her stomach.

"Shhh, no matter," Minton assured, caressing her face. Inwardly he hated John Jr. "Mama Lotti can take care of her, and you and I, we can start over." *Have some babies of our own.* He felt John Jr. stole moments that should have been theirs together. "I love you; I can't live without you. I can't." He felt free finally owning up to his harbored emotions. He'd loved Puah from day one. "Nothing else matters to me. Let's start over. Mama Lotti will take good care of her. I'll send her money to help, I will. I won't feel any differently about you. I love you, Pu."

Puah knew it was wrong, but she could never love Rahab as Lotti did. Although she felt horrible about considering Minton's plan and fought with herself, hope began to surface in her heart. She couldn't help getting excited about New York, seeing Mags again, and the fluttering she felt whenever Minton spoke. Puah loved Lotti, but it was no secret that they *beat to a different drum.* Lotti had dreams for her that weren't her own. Puah wanted sparks, romance, and the finer things in life; whereas, Lotti was content with working hard and living quietly. Puah, on the other hand, needed rescuing and Minton was her hero. She wasn't going to allow him to fly off without her.

Later that night, while everyone slept, Puah snuck into Lotti's chest and took cash from a deposit envelope. She also stole her mother's savings account booklet. *It's for my education anyway.* She tucked the stolen money safely into her packed suitcase then left the bayou home she never acquainted. Minton met her a half mile up the road. They stayed for the rest of the evening in the hotel outside of town until the bank opened in the morning. Minton knew that his supposed fiancé's father was on a manhunt for him, but he slept peacefully with Puah in his arms.

Puah convinced herself out of the plagued depression, considering it best to live the life she was given if she couldn't have the life she wanted with Daphne. Her feelings for Minton were different. She presumed she wasn't in love with him, but she liked him enough to get along. He was a kind, smart, strong, dependable man who would faithfully provide for her. She decided she would allow him to spoil her in the manner which she was accustomed. *Maybe in time, I'll grow to love him as he deserves? Until then, I'll woo him of any regrets.*

After years of courting, Puah allowed her heart to beat against Minton's rhythm. He knew her, and she was safe with him. It felt natural to consummate their relationship beyond friendship.

THE SOUTH BRONX

Lotti painfully vowed Puah out of her life forever; she had added *insult to injury* by moving in with Mags and Richard upon arriving in New York City. Ashamed, Puah called Lotti apologizing. She explained that she needed a fresh start and revealed that she was with Minton and staying with Mags until settled.

I hope Mama can't hear the joy in my voice. I'm glad she can't see this smile across my face that Minton painted with his kisses.

Minton made Puah feel alive again, and she felt guilty for that.

Puah inquired no information regarding Rahab. There was a silent agreement of adoption between her and Lotti. Lotti knew Rahab was a painful reminder and she understood why Puah left. However, she had a hard time understanding how she could *toss the baby out with the bathwater.*

In spite of Lotti's feelings, Mags and Puah picked up where they left off, not skipping a beat. They acted the same toward one another, but they both had changed. Puah matured, carrying too much luggage for a young woman to bear, while prison changed Mags. The upbeat spirit of the dancing girl from Baton Rouge eluded her. Mags drank heavily and often displayed split personalities that bordered psychotic.

Mags ran number-holes and whorehouses when the days of hustling magic potions and selling the twirl of her hips were long behind her. The big bands of the 1950s and 60s that she and Richard once gained notability with had

56

long gone out of style. Their dreams of 'taking a bite out of the Big Apple' turned on them. Out of desperation, Mags turned to prostitution while Richard, determined not to give up on his music, played his sax in any nightclub that would let him through the door.

Although he had never met her, when Puah walked into Richard and Mags' beautiful, historic brownstone on Strivers Row in Harlem, Richard felt a bit emotional. Right away he noticed their similar features. They were both tall, lean, and wrapped in lightly creamed caramel coatings. Puah's deep-set eyes sparkled like Mags and Lotti's. Her full lips curled into the brightest smile he'd seen in a long time. New York City women were hard and cold. Puah was fresh out of the bayou; her innocence was refreshing. The emotional glitch Richard initially felt quickly reversed into perverse desires.

Minton and Puah hadn't stayed a month before Minton noticed Richard's lustful gawking. He hugged and rubbed Puah longer than a father should. It was obvious to Minton that he and Richard were going to bump heads. Although Minton was impressed by Richard's business knowledge and street savoir-faire he knew it was time for he and Puah to leave.

Richard introduced Minton to a few reliable business contacts and Minton bought his first property in the South Bronx. It was a storefront with an overhead two-bedroom apartment. He read somewhere in a business magazine that the South Bronx, falling victim to arson and rampant crime, was virtually abandoned. The lack of city services plus the relinquishment and neglect of landlords left the once predominantly Jewish community invisible.

In Minton's eyes, he saw an opportunity for reestablishment for those strong enough to wade the storm. He remembered the stories his parents shared about how they survived the floods. Instead of relocating like most people, they took everything they had and bought cheap property. They persevered and used good old-fashioned intuitiveness to press through the hard times. Eventually, they accomplished their goals, and Minton reaped the benefits.

Having money and feeling lucky to have Puah by his side, Minton bought the cheap South Bronx property. He also purchased two purebred docked-tailed Doberman Pinschers, a *Smith & Wesson,* and a sawed-off shotgun. To push the progress of the rebuilding of his investments, Minton joined informal coalitions and community development groups. He sent for his state-of-the-art dry cleaning equipment from storage and traded his *Ford F100* for a service van. Then he started his first *pick-up and delivery* dry cleaning business, serving all of the Bronx and parts of Harlem.

That first month in the Bronx, Puah and Minton hardly slept. The thunderous chug of the *IRT* number 2 and 5 trains coming down White Plains Road kept them awake. The screeching metal brakes had them twisting and turning in bed. Approaching trains blasted their horns and startled them if they dozed. The annoying *bong* signal of closing doors let them know it was safe to rest until the next train.

Soon the blending sounds of transit, gunshots, yelling, and music became the melody of city nights. They were as soothing as cricket's chirping and toads croaking, and they couldn't sleep without them.

Puah wished that Minton had purchased a home in Harlem closer to Mags and Richard where she felt safe, but Minton promised they'd make more of a profit if they lived above the business. He and the dogs, King and Queen, would protect her and the business. Puah trusted Minton with all of her heart. If anything he was truthful, but old habits die hard. She found the nearest *Santeria Botanica* and had charmed amulets made for their protection.

Minton honored his promises. After the storm of the first few years came the pot of gold at the end of the rainbow. He was able to keep Puah draped in jewelry and dressed *to the nines* as she was accustomed. The couple lived comfortably and enjoyed the culture of city life. When the business turned a profit, he bought more vans and hired drivers. Minton preferred working locally; there he could develop his business and the community, and stay close to home.

Puah, who seemed to show up in New York City already pregnant, honored Lotti's wishes and used most of the stolen money to attend nursing school. She, not particularly liking the gamble of running a business, figured if all else failed they'd have her career to fall on. *Charlotte Auguste didn't raise a complete fool.*

The young couple welcomed a bouncing baby boy nine months after arriving in the city. They named him Minton Silas Williams, Jr. Minton, once being a junior himself, wanted his son to carry on his name. However, because of the strained relationship he had with his deceased father, he chose to reset the descendancy, calling himself the senior and his son the junior.

Three years later, Puah gave birth to a daughter, and Minton honored his late mother by naming the baby after her. Elizabeth Gomer Williams. Both he and Puah addressed the children by their middle names and nicknamed them Si and Go-Go.

Two kids, two dogs, two dry cleaning businesses, and a nursing degree later, Minton and Puah were able to pay down on their first home. As part of the rebuilding and formalization plans of the South Bronx, Charlotte Street was chosen as *the face of rebirth*. Minton and Puah owned a piece of history.

J.C. MILLER

RAHAB

THE BOILING POT

Steaming hot white linen hangs, drenching wet, above her head. The fragrance of Big Mama's signature scent of rosemary and lavender oil drifts through the dense swampy air. The chanting song of cicadas, accompanied by the throaty hymn of bullfrogs, competes with the rolling sound of boiling water. Rahab wonders, while positioning herself between dripping sheets shielding her from the blazing Louisiana sun, *Is Big Mama the only person on earth who still hand washes, boils, and presses linen? It is 1982.* The anticipation of the duties still left to be done torments her. Fidgeting and feeling suffocated by the heat, she hands Big Mama more wooden pins from a worn wicker basket. With little focus, she tries to make sense of what the noblewoman is mumbling through the pins gathered in her mouth. *Creole rambling.* She guesses it is not necessarily intended for an 11-year-old granddaughter.

Big Mama's words seem to float through the air on the heat waves. Her gestures and smiling eyes make up for the lack of conversation.

She looks like a melting candy bar. Rahab giggles while wiping her own sweaty brow with the back of her hand. *I wish I was at the lake.* She grimaces and scratches at the hives welting around her arm. *I'll take fifty itchy rashes over laundry any day*

"Told ya to rub down wit dat ointment, gal," Big Mama mumbles, glancing at her fidgety, flushed-faced granddaughter. "A hard head makes a soft behind...or a

62

swollen arm in ya case," she chuckles, keeping to her work.

"Big Mama, how much mo' left?" Rahab whines, rubbing the inside of her itchy arm against her faded denim overalls.

Big Mama pauses and, with bulging, dark chestnut eyes, gives her granddaughter "*the look.*" "Hmph, you got better places to be? Lak back down to de bog, huh? You got better ways to make dis here money?" She sucks her tongue against her teeth. "Hand me some mo' of dem pins, gal."

"Other kids probably watching TV or sumphin. Why ah gotta be stuck here?" Rahab asks, shoving more pins into her grandmother's reaching hands.

Big Mama pauses again, placing her full fists on her hips. "Watch yo'self naw," she warns. "Ah ain't got no *other kids* so ah don't much care 'bout what dey do. But dis one here..." She taps a pin against Rahab's chest, and then back toward her own, "she mine, and she fixin' to be somebody." Returning to her work, she continues to fuss. "She ain't gone be sitting around all day watching TV either. Going blind and keeping silly notions. No, ma'am. She gone be a doctor. Ain't dat right?" Big Mama smugly predicts.

Rahab sighs and rolls her eyes. "Dis ain't fair."

Big Mama chuckles. "Fair? Chile, fair is for white folks. You gotta earn ya way in dis here world." She glances at Rahab again with "*the look,*" then slowly states, "Or be owned. You wanna be owned by sum gov'ment, some jailhouse, or worse...some man?" Big Mama laughs at the notion. She places the clothespins back into her mouth and mumbles in a thick Louisiana Creole accent.

Rahab sighs, shaking her head. A debate over not becoming a doctor would only result in losing against Big Mama. She decides it's too hot to be lectured; the less she speaks, the quicker she can get to fishing with Salmone.

Salmone, Pastor Josh's son, is more like a brother than a friend. He and Rahab were raised together. When Rahab isn't with Big Mama she spends her time fishing with him. Pastor Josh and his family have gained Lotti's trust over the years. Rahab is allowed to go almost anywhere with them except for The House of Judah. Whenever Rahab mentions attending the church, Lotti journeys into one of her terrifying stories from her past.

She eerily repeats what her own grandmother said to her when she was a child and would plead to attend a church service. "Ah knows all too well of dey lyin' tongues, cutting words, and fancy Bibles. Dem books is what trapped de ancestors in slavery, don't ya know? Drove our magic deep in da woods and deeper in de by'you in de first place. Dey not worried 'bout us learning no Bibles, beb. Dey worried 'bout dey secrets being told. Dey want my magic at night, in de dark. Den serve dey god in de light for all eyes to see how holy dey is. A pack of wolves!"

Lotti never explains why Rahab can't participate in any church activities, she only states, "Round here, de church and Voodoo is lak o'l and water, but in de closet, dey sugar and spice. Follow ya own path, Rah. If dey church is on it, it'll find ya. Till den, we our own religion."

J.C. MILLER

SUN SET

"Aba, daba, daba, daba, daba, daba, dab,"
Said the Chimpie to the Monk.
"Baba, daba, daba, daba, daba, daba, dab,"
Said the Monkey to the Chimp.
All night long they'd chatter away,
All day long they're happy and gay,
Swinging and singing in their hunky, tonkey way.

Rahab sings, pedaling up a steep hedge-lined driveway. Panting heavily, she finishes the entire nursery rhyme before reaching the top. By the end of summer, she intends on reaching the top of the driveway before ending the song. Besides that, it gives her something other to do than think of the dreaded laundry chores. She hates delivering the cleaned sheets as much as she hates hanging them. Quickly, she distributes each package and collects payments while Lotti drives slowly behind her, up and down the street Lotti nicknamed *Money Mile.*

House number one is the Lawson *abode.* Rahab likes the Lawsons. She thinks they're pretty nice for rich white folks. They prefer to personally hand Rahab their payments instead of having *the help* do it, and they always offer her a treat before she leaves.

House number two belongs to Mrs. Dupree, the cat lady. Since her husband's passing, she's taken to collecting cats. The late Mr. Dupree was severely allergic to them and Mrs. Dupree, having owned cats throughout her childhood, missed having them around. There's a rumor that she now owns nearly fifty felines. Lotti's scented linen, as well as her deodorizing spray, are needed to freshen this home.

House number three is the Alexandre's *Maison*, overly adorned in puffy pink ruffles, thick burgundy velvet, and trimmed in gold leaf. Their French maid, Miss Lulu, deems Rahab as a toddler.

"Aren't you the cutest little thing," she shrieks, pinching Rahab's cheeks and tousling her hair.

Rahab can't stand it. When Salmone heard of the torturing, he gave Rahab one of his baseball caps to cover her head. Now when Miss Lulu answers the door, Rahab's ready. She places the cap on before ringing the bell and puffs her cheeks out. Unfortunately, Miss Lulu gets a hoot out of that. She laughs, cupping Rahab's face and says, "You are so cute!"

House number four is Dr. Chester's estate. Rahab doesn't like delivering there at all. She thinks it's creepy and so is Dr. Chester with his glass eye, for that matter. When he looks at Rahab, she can see her reflection straight through the prosthetic, and it makes her feel uncomfortable. She's certain he's a robot in disguise. In public, Dr. Chester covers the glass eye with a patch, but Rahab's on to him.

On this particular task driven day, Dr. Chester's help, Nancy, runs down the driveway yelling for Lotti.

"Ms. Lotti, Ms. Lotti! One of ya babies is coming. Dey needs ya at de Beaumont Estate right away," she informs Lotti, barely stopping to breathe. "Dr. Chester said if ya agree, ah can help de chile finish up ya route den take her on home for ya?" Nancy adds, running alongside the car as Lotti pulls into the driveway.

Lotti accepts the doctor's generosity and asks that Rahab is dropped off at Salmone's family's home instead. She doesn't fancy leaving her rambunctious 11-year-old home alone, especially not knowing what time she'll finish at the Beaumont Estate.

Once Lotti hands off the remaining packages and instructs her granddaughter to behave, she leaves. Rahab, standing at the top of the driveway, waves until her grandmother is out of sight. The unexpected change in plans brightens the outlook of an otherwise ordinary day for her. She can hardly wait to finish the deliveries.

It's almost evening and that means plenty of catfish to be caught.

"Come in, chile, while ah fetch my keys," Nancy orders from the doorway, interrupting Rahab's daydreaming.

Rahab hurriedly drops her bike near the packages and enters the house curious about its interior.

"Naw don't ya touch anything," Nancy demands, ushering her through the entryway and giving her a quick once-over. She notices Rahab's raggedy sneakers. "Ah sure hope those tenny shoes are clean, ah just passed da mop dis morning."

"Yes, ma'am," Rahab answers. *I sure hope they're clean too.*

She catches a glimpse of her reflection plainly cast upon the massive slabs of glistening white marble covering the floor and wipes the worn sneakers off on each other just in case.

Before Nancy can leave to collect her keys, Dr. Chester appears walking gracefully down the spiral staircase as though floating.

"Is that my package, Nancy?"

"Why yes, sir, it is. Ah was just 'bout to put it in de linen closet and fetch my keys. Ms.—"

Dr. Chester cuts Nancy off, addressing Rahab. "I love your grandmother's work. Her sheets aren't stiff like others and the scent is...heavenly, for lack of a better word," he says, sort of smirking as he reaches the landing and approaches the women in the foyer. He reaches for the package from Nancy. "Nancy, please go ask Edgar to bring the car around. I'll be assisting Miss Auguste on her route. It's a lovely time of the day for a cruise."

"Yes, sir, it is, but ah done told Ms. Lotti, I'd take de chile," Nancy nervously responds, handing him the linen that is neatly wrapped in brown paper and twine.

Dr. Chester inhales the scent coming from the bundle. "Mmm, yes marvelous," he declares, winking at Rahab.

He isn't wearing a patch over his eye. Rahab swallows hard and attempts to return the smile.

"Yes, Nancy, I'm aware of the situation," Dr. Chester states, now directing his attention toward her. "However, you're now free to finish your work."

His face is stern, and Nancy knows that his change of plans requires no explanations.

"Thank ya, sir." She nods, quickly leaving to find his driver.

Dr. Chester clears his throat and attempts to smile. "Okay, young lady, allow me to fetch my jacket, and we'll be on our way." He awkwardly nods his head, clears his throat again, then turns to leave. "There's candy in the crystal dish on the console table. Please help yourself; I'll be right back," he adds, turning slightly as he walks away.

"Yes, thank you," Rahab answers, standing as still as a statue until he disappears behind the staircase.

Exhaling, she relaxes her shoulders and twirls on her heels toward the designated candy dish. *I can't believe how beautiful this house is.* She pauses to admire a crystal chandelier suspended above her head.

To Rahab, everything looks expensive and screams *caution, do not touch!* The tall walls are sheathed in fabric and have naked statues displayed all along them. The white marble flooring looks like a frozen lake, and Rahab desperately wants to run and slide across it, but, not wanting to get in any trouble, she fights off the notion.

She brushes her hands over her overalls then mindfully opens the crystal bowl containing fancy assorted hard candy. She pops one or two in her mouth then proceeds to take enough for herself, Salmone, and his grandmother, Ms. Ruby. Carefully, she places the lid back on the dish.

"Hello," she says, listening for an echo.

It's her first time in the main house. She usually collects payments from Nancy at the kitchen door or from Dr. Chester when he's pruning his beloved roses on the front lawn. Rahab enjoys running in circles through the perfumed maze shaped garden. Her heart races with fear knowing Dr. Chester's lurking somewhere in there. He jumps out at her every time, then dangles an envelope from his gloved hand. A crooked smile lays slanted on his face as if saying, *"Come and get it if you dare."*

"Did you find any you like?" Dr. Chester asks, reappearing from behind the stairs. He's wearing a navy-blue duster and a black patch over his eye.

"Yes, sir," Rahab mumbles through the candy gathered in her mouth.

"Excellent. Let's be on our way."

Dr. Chester drives slowly down *Money Mile* nodding at the nosy neighbors who recognize his car as Rahab delivers the remaining linen packages.

"He looks lak de king of Mardi Gras," she whispers to herself.

All of Lotti's patrons meet Rahab at their front doors with their payments in hand, instead of sending their *help* to pay her from the kitchen doors as usual.

"Where's your grandmother, child?" they all ask through fake smiles and clenched teeth, staring past Rahab down their driveways at Dr. Chester.

"Is she okay?" they question, obviously uninterested.

"Hello, Dr. Chester! How very kind of you to accommodate this poor child. He's such a good man. Make sure you thank him properly, you here?" they demand, shutting their doors in her face before she can respond.

When the errand of laundry is complete, Dr. Chester patiently follows Rahab's pointed out directions to Salmone's house.

"It has been quite a pleasure driving you today, Miss Auguste."

"Thank you, Mister Dr. Chester."

He awkwardly smirks. "I've been thinking. My workers at the orchard could use some extra help picking in the evening. It would be an incredible opportunity for a young girl to earn some wages. Wouldn't you agree?"

"Oh yes, sir! I'd lak dat very much," Rahab shrieks, practically bouncing in her seat. "I'm a good picker and ah can climb high too."

70

The possibility of getting away from the house and sheets for the rest of the summer is exciting. For a second, Dr. Chester has two healthy eyes and isn't creepy.

"Great!" he responds, glancing down at her naked leg. He extends a hand and lightly pats her thigh.

Rahab feels uncomfortable. She tugs down on her overall shorts. Lotti just mentioned the other day that she was *"growing faster than an old ivy vine."*

"I'll work out the arrangements with your grandmother," he states, bringing his hand back to the steering wheel.

"Da house is here!" Rahab yells before he misses it.

The old white house with the enclosed screen porch never looked so welcoming. The only thing missing is Ms. Ruby. She usually sits in her rocker waiting in hopes of a passer-by to shoot the breeze with. Rahab opens the car door before Dr. Chester parks. She can hardly wait to get out.

"Wait! Before you go," Dr. Chester yells, grabbing her arm. "Your grandmother mentioned that you're interested in the medical field. She said that you would like to become a doctor."

Rahab smiles, trying not to be rude and make *stinky faces* as Lotti calls them.

"Did you know that I worked at St. Hope Hospital for over forty years? I was the chief surgeon over my department."

"No, sir," Rahab bitterly answers.

"Yes, I also lecture at universities, but I can barely keep up with that nowadays. My point, before I lose myself is, I would like to share some of my books and notes with you. You can be my young apprentice." He rubs her shoulder.

Rahab shrugs and he snickers.

"Oh, sweet Rahab. You have the face of an angel." He palms her chin as though studying her. She makes the *stinky face* in disapproval. "I never found the time to marry and have children - my study was my love. Alas, time has escaped me," he continues, coming from a trance. "Well, off you go before I grow too sentimental."

"Yes, sir! Bye, Dr. Chester."

Rahab races out of the car. Her stomach feels funny.

"Don't forget your bike!" Dr. Chester yells, noticing it laying across the back seat.

Rahab sighs and twirls around.

"It doesn't look like anyone is home." He points out as she approaches. He surveys the area. "I don't see any cars or lights. Are you sure they're home?"

Rahab's afraid to answer. She might throw up. The thought crossed her mind when she noticed Ms. Ruby wasn't in her usual spot.

Dr. Chester exits the car, walks up the yard, and rings the bell. He's acting strange and making Rahab feel more uncomfortable than usual. She wants to run but the thought of Lotti *tanning her hide* as she often threatens keeps her.

After ringing and knocking a few times more, he turns and says, "I guess it's you and me, kiddo."

Rahab's stomach drops.

"I'll stay here on de porch. Someone will be home soon. Maybe dey at church. Mr. Abrams is a pastor you know?"

She drops her bike and heads for the porch.

"Don't be ridiculous. You're my responsibility. I'll take you back to my house and we'll leave a message for your grandmother at the Beaumont residence."

The daunting day bursts into a vivid ending. Radiant colors dance through the evening sky as Dr. Chester drives along slowly in deep thought.

"What a lovely sunset!" he yells, as though discovering it suddenly. "Let's get out and watch," he suggests, making a sharp turn toward the lake.

"Ah don't tink we should. My Big Mama might worry." *Where are you, Big Mama?*

"No worries. We have some time to spare."

Dr. Chester parks in the thick of some bushes.

"We'll only be a few minutes. Besides, it's a sin, possibly the greatest, not to notice God in the midst of His work."

He exits, and Rahab considers locking herself in. *No telling how long it'll be before someone comes along.* She and Salmone fish and play at the lake unbothered for hours. *He could kill and bury me before anyone shows up.*

The doctor opens Rahab's door and gently takes her hand. He attempts smiling to put her at ease, but it looks painful. Rahab exits the car, and, hand-in-hand, they stroll along the shoreline.

Dr. Chester inhales deeply and states, "Delightful. Simply marvelous."

He notices an oddly placed picnic table and bench. Pastor Josh put it there for cleaning fish. The First Lady loves seafood but she hates the mess her husband makes cleaning them. Rahab and Dr. Chester walk over, and he sits.

"Look at God's work! Breathtaking isn't it? God paints a new masterpiece each day for us all to enjoy."

Rahab never considered such a thing and notices the twilight in a new way.

Brilliant hues twirl untainted in the heavens. The setting sun appears halved against the horizon until it kisses the lake and magically appears whole again. Rahab gasps in amazement at nature reflecting itself upon the water. She can't believe she's never stopped to notice.

Maybe I'm wrong about him? She turns to thank him for the experience. His eye is moist and red from crying. Tears roll from under his eye patch, and Rahab makes a mental note to notify Salmone that glass eyes cry tears. Dr. Chester tugs her arm, drawing her closer to him.

"Relax. Sit here on my lap."

"No thanks, I'll stand." She pulls away, reconfirming her need to worry.

He smirks. *The kid's got spirit.* "You know, if I had a daughter, I'd want her to be like you. Do you know your father?"

"No," Rahab mutters.

Tears fill her eyes for no necessary reason, other than it's a sensitive subject. Besides, if she knew her father, she would tell on Dr. Chester. If she knew her father, he would give him two glass eyes. If she knew her father, she wouldn't be at the lake feeling scared and alone.

"Oh, dear child, sit on my lap. Don't cry. I'm an old, lonely, half-blind man. Do entertain my simple wishes. Don't be afraid."

He guides her down on his knee. Rahab sits facing the sun as it waves goodbye.

"Goodbye sun," she whispers.

Dr. Chester wraps his arms around her waist and begins to quote a poem by *Emily Dickinson.*

"Bring me the sunset in a cup,
Reckon the morning's flagons up
And say how many Dew,
Tell me how far the morning leaps
Tell me what time the weaver sleeps
Who spun the breadth of blue..."

Rahab stares aimlessly off into the horizon, trying not to think and trying not to feel the bulge growing through Dr. Chester's expensive trousers underneath her. His beautiful words become short and unclear between heavy breathing.

Feeling anxious, Rahab tries to sing. "Aba, daba, daba..." but the words escape her memory.

She can feel her spirit rising out of her panicked body. It floats away in an escape and intertwines with the colors of twilight.

"Come back," she whispers but Dr. Chester's panting drowns her plea.

His hands are all over her, feeling, touching, grabbing, and kneading her body. Lotti's warning comes to Rahab's mind. *"Don't let dem dirty boys touch ya treasure box, beb. Babies are born and aborted from de treasure box."* Rahab is aware of what Lotti does when the young girls come crying at night. Some come alone. Some come with their mothers. Very few, come with gentlemen friends. Some aren't young girls at all.

A knot the size and texture of a field mouse blocks Rahab's throat, she feels woozy. She closes her eyes and clenches her fist as tight as she can. She can't get Lotti's bloody tools and towels out of her mind. *Am I getting pregnant?*

"Please, Mister Doctor," she whispers. *What is he doing?*

Dr. Chester fiddles with his pant zipper, trying to free the growing bulge. The knot in Rahab's throat raises but just before it forces her mouth open into a scream - he thrusts her away from him.

Falling to her hands and knees, Rahab quickly looks back, wanting to keep him in her sight. His face is flushed.

"Don't...look...at...me!" Dr. Chester yells in a demonic tone.

Rahab quickly turns away and closes her eyes. His moans grow louder as he sits pleasuring himself.

Afraid to move, Rahab tucks her head, trembling and crying uncontrollably. She wishes she knew a spell to cast on him.

From now on I'll listen to Big Mama. I'll watch her when she works and be the witch doctor's granddaughter. From now on, I'll hate sunsets forever.

DR. JEKYLL AND MR. HYDE

The trip back to Dr. Chester's mansion is quiet. Rahab points out directions into town. She manages to stop crying and sits in silence trying to understand what happened at the lake. Feelings of hate and pity toward Dr. Chester conflict within her. He continuously apologizes, stating that he's a sick old man as he sniffles and blows at his red, running nose. Rahab's not sure why he's crying, but she knows what he did was wrong. He touched her where he ought not and was *scary and rough. Now he's pathetic. How could this pitiful looking man want to hurt me? Why did he? Maybe he wants a daughter that looks like me?* The possibility of pregnancy makes her feel sick. *Maybe if I find him a wife, he'll be happy and leave me alone. How about Ms. Lulu, the French maid? No, Ms. Nancy, she'll have little mixed babies that look like me.*

Before Rahab can conjure up a plan to get the two interested in each other, the car slows down. They were a few blocks away from *Money Mile.* Dr. Chester turns toward her. Speaking in a deliberate cold tone, he says, "We must never speak a word of this."

He pushes his patch up on his forehead and stares directly at her instead of the road. The car wobbles under his misdirected attention.

"I would hate for your grandmother to lose her business or home. Believe me; I don't want that to happen. However, if our secret gets out? I'll have no choice in the matter. All of those neighbors you saw today would side with me."

Rahab remembers all of his waves and nodding earlier. The king of Money Mile. *How could I have felt pity for him? He's Dr. Jekyll and Mr. Hyde.*

"You see, Rahab, no one would believe you. I'm a doctor; you're just a kid. The granddaughter of a witch doctor." Rahab clenches her fists in anger. "You both would have to leave town, and Lotti would never work again. Understood?" he asks as they turn into his driveway.

"Yes, sir," Rahab manages to answer, fighting back tears. *He's right.* She recalls all the stories Big Mama told her. *The townspeople killed The Grandmother,* she remembers, fearing for their lives.

Edgar, Dr. Chester's driver, meets them at the top of the driveway. He swiftly walks over to open Dr. Chester's door. "Evening, sir."

"Good evening, Edgar. Take Miss Auguste into the kitchen and tell the cook to ring her grandmother at the Beaumont Estate. Inform her that her granddaughter is still here. No one answered at the Abrams' residence."

Dr. Chester slightly turns his head toward the car to bid Rahab goodnight but instead clears his throat and walks away - disappearing behind the grand mahogany doors.

J.C. MILLER

GREY'S ANATOMY

Before I formed you in the belly, I knew you.
Before you came forth out of the womb, I sanctified you.
Jeremiah 1:5

Rahab lays in the back of a rusty old pickup truck with her arms folded behind her head. A clear blue yonder sets the backdrop to her thoughts.

Who is this God that paints the sky? Who spun the breadth of blue?

She stares at nothing, in particular, recalling Dr. Chester's poem. *Where is God hiding?* She questions, trying to imagine the magnitude of the universe, God's greatness, and her importance as a speck in it all. The complex awakening brings a tear to her eye.

"Why is he hiding?" Rahab whispers.

"Wha'cha say now?" Laura-Ann, Rahab's travel companion asks as she pulls colorful strings of yarn from a tote bag.

"Nothing, just thinking out loud."

"Oh, talking to ya'self, huh? You must gone be rich," Laura-Ann chuckles, continuing to crochet.

Dr. Chester followed through on his word and asked Lotti if Rahab could pick at his orchard. Lotti hesitated at first, having a busy schedule herself. She had no time to drive Rahab around. So, Dr. Chester suggested that Rahab ride in with a group of pickers who came through the bayou. He even volunteered to make the arrangements. He left no room for Lotti to say no; except she wondered why all of the sudden the interest in her granddaughter. Dr.

Chester added, "When you drop off the linen you can pick up a few medical books for Rahab to borrow. She's a brilliant young lady."

That was the deal maker for Lotti.

Three weeks and two days had passed since Rahab started picking at the orchard. Three weeks and four days had passed since the terrible and horrible unspoken day. Rahab is maneuvering through her once ordinary life like a balloon on a short string. As in dreams where complications interrupt your ability to fly adequately, she's slightly hovering. She sees everything differently now, from the perspective of a balloon on a short string suspended in the air. She's present but owns no weight. People haven't changed. Things haven't changed. Rahab has changed. Maybe it's because her soul up and left; it was too scared to stay, or maybe it's because she doesn't know if she's pregnant or not?

Rahab tightly closes her eyes. In her mind, she can hear Lotti preaching to the young girls who come searching for her help.

"Dis is what happens when ya too fo'ward. When ya can't wait till de proper time. You let dem greedy boys fool ya. Let'em have de milk without buying de cow. Den ya ends up with babies ya can't keep. Mama knows, Mama knows. I'ma fix it fuh ya, ah sho' is."

How can Big Mama fix it for me if I can't tell her what happened? What will happen when I start to show? Rahab worries about thoughts too complicated for an 11-year-old to solve. She opens her eyes and through blurred vision examines Laura-Ann's stomach.*I hope to be like her.*

Laura-Ann is Rahab's new friend, traveling companion, and co-worker at the orchard and she is very much pregnant. Laura-Ann is in her sixth month and hardly shows. Rahab would have never known if she hadn't asked, *"Who are you making a blanket for?"*

Laura-Ann proudly patted her stomach and revealed, *"It's fuh da baby in my belly."*

Ever since that moment, Rahab's become obsessed with her. She studies how Laura-Ann picks berries, and how she walks, stands, and rubs her lower back. She even knows how often Laura-Ann frequents the port-a-potty.

About a week ago, Rahab conjured up the nerve and curiously asked, "Laura-Ann, ah know dat babies come from de woman's toochie, but how dey get up der and how dey stay put without falling out?"

Laura-Ann laughed so hard she nearly wet herself.

"Well, ah suppose you gone have to ask ya ma 'bout dat tonight. It ain't my place to say," she answered, taking Rahab's hand and placing it on her belly.

Something jumped like a bullfrog caught in her stomach.

"Ooh!" Rahab squealed in amazement.

"De baby is laughing too," Laura-Ann claimed.

It's one week later and Rahab still has no answers or bullfrogs jumping in her belly. She also hasn't seen or heard from Dr. Chester, but every night she has nightmares of him torturing her at the orchard. The anxiety of not knowing his next move binds her stomach into knots. She tries to lose herself in monotonous work, but everything's changed.

One evening, Dr. Chester's car pulled up at the orchard. Rahab spotted it from a distance as it came up the road. In fear, she jumped up from her work and haphazardly began to run in circles, knocking over buckets of berries and alerting the other pickers. Concerned, Laura-Ann grabbed her by the arms and held her firm. Rahab started to cry but noticed Dr. Chester's driver, Edgar, exiting the car. He came to deliver her a beautiful leather-bound book titled, *Grey's Anatomy* along with a few of Dr. Chester's notebooks containing handwritten notes. Embarrassed yet still physically shaken, Rahab apologized to everyone saying she saw a garter snake then returned to work.

When Rahab got home that night, she thumbed through the book searching for information to unleash the mystery of *where babies come from*, but the technical terms used were like a foreign language to the 11-year-old. *No wonder!* She examined the book's cover. *This book was published in 1918*

"Ah didn't even know dey had books back den," she said out loud, stumbling upon a chapter titled, *Embryology.*

The chapter spoke of the human reproductive organs, germinal vesicles, *Spermatozoöns,* and the fetus, all of which were French to Rahab. She studied the sketched drawings and gathered that a woman gets pregnant when thousands of tiny tadpoles swim into something that looks like a goat's head with large horns. The tadpoles attack an egg, and the egg grows into an embryo. *What's an em-bry-o?* She didn't recall any of that happening with Dr. Chester. *We were at the lake though...and there's a pretty good chance that tadpoles were in the water. But what does that have to do with a woman's treasure box?* Rahab was sure that Dr. Chester touched hers and no goats, tadpoles, or eggs were involved. The book only made her more confused.

After dinner, Rahab showed Lotti what she was reading. Big Mama took the book and turned to the last page. "Start from here, beb, and when you get back to here..." she flipped to the first page, "den you'll understand better. If not, I'll be ready to explain."

"Big Mama, ders over one-thousand pages in dis book! It'll be next summer by time ah finish. Besides, de words is too hard."

"You smart. Doctors gotta know er'rything, from de rooter to de tooter. No skipping 'round when it comes to de body. But till den, you just remember not to let dem dirty behind boys mess with ya cat, ya hear?" Lotti replied, giving Rahab *the look* and shoving the book back in her hands.

"Yes'm," Rahab mumbled, disappointed. She turned and walked back to her room then placed the humongous book on her dresser and never touched it again.

THE UNSPOKEN

"Bye, Laura-Ann! Bye, Ms. Sadie! Bye, Red-man, Mr. Foy!" Rahab yells, standing off the road, waving at the rusty old pickup truck as it drove away.

On Fridays, Rahab sleeps over at Salmone's house. Lotti does her counseling, potions, and seances until Saturday afternoon.

Rahab thought she wanted to learn Voodoo, but the first Friday after the *unspoken day* proved to be enough learning for her. When she saw Lotti's knife barely graze the breast of a live chicken, then dark red blood oozing over its white feathers, she gagged and excused herself. Wearing one of Lotti's charmed amulets seemed more appealing after that.

"Hey, der, Rah, beb! What's cooking, good-looking?" Ms. Ruby, Salmone's grandmother, questions from her rocker on the porch. "You made ya'self some money today, huh? Let me loan some."

Rahab smirks and kisses the older woman on her forehead.

"Awrite, how you?" she answers, dryly.

"Ooh, fair to middlin'. But you don't look too good today. Dey workin ya too hard?"

"No'm, just tired is all," Rahab lies, rubbing her eyes and yawning.

"You sure er'rything is alright? Ah don't see ya springin' up de yard and runnin through dat ol' screen door lak ya used to, gal. What's ailing ya?" Ms. Ruby continues with a concern in her voice that touches Rahab's heart.

Rahab tries to hold back tears, but a sharp pain is stabbing at her chest. She begins to sob. She hasn't cried since the unspoken day, and the outburst feels good.

"Oh, der, der, sugah. It's gonna be alright," Ms. Ruby assures, rubbing Rahab's back. "Sit on down," she insists, patting her legs.

Rahab plops into Ms. Ruby's lap and buries her face into the older woman's shoulder. She smells of mothballs and menthol. Ms. Ruby cradles her in her arms and rocks for a while, humming nothing in particular.

"How old is ya naw, beb? Let's see Sal is thirteen nearly fourteen, so dat makes you..." Ms. Ruby begins to count.

"I'm eleven, be twelve in two weeks," Rahab states, cutting in.

"Ooh, ah see naw!" Ms. Ruby shouts as if she's discovered a secret. "You done start ya friend yet, chile?"

"Oh, no, ma'am! Ah ain't on no rags." Rahab sits up, wiping tears from her cheeks.

"Den dat's it. It's sho'nuf gonna come, ah guarantee! Probably before summer's out," Ms. Ruby predicts.

"Oh, please no. Don't say dat. Ah don't want no Tante Flo visiting no time soon," Rahab laughs, waving her arms and hands, *NO*.

Ms. Ruby laughs. "You is moody, dat's all. Sho'is a hard ting fuh us women...dat and birthing babies. We can't seem to catch a break, ah tell ya da truth."

Rahab lays her head back down on Ms. Ruby's shoulder, then asks as sweet as pie, "Maw-Maw Ruby, where do babies come from?"

Ms. Ruby coughs and chokes in astonishment. She pushes and swats Rahab off of her lap.

85

"You okay?" Rahab questions, patting the older woman's back.

Ms. Ruby retrieves a handkerchief from her bosom and wipes her eyes and mouth. "Gone, gal!" she insists. "You almost made me choke on my teets." She waves Rahab away. "Sal's waiting for ya at de lake anyhow."

"But, ah just—" Rahab tries to ask again.

"You know de stork bring dem babies. Now choo!" Ms. Ruby waves. "Made me choke on my teets," she repeats, mumbling to herself.

Rahab runs off of the porch, out of the yard, and down the matted road. She runs the entire distance, moving as swift as she can. She runs to feel the evening air rush against her hot skin. She runs because it feels like escaping. She runs knowing that Salmone will be mad at her. Then she runs even faster.

For the past few weeks, Rahab has been a disappointment to Salmone. She's broken a few play dates, and when they're together, she's not herself. She's distant and moody. Since she started picking at the orchard, the friends barely have time to fish anymore. Not that Rahab wants to visit the lake, but fishing is their favorite pastime.

Salmone has noticed the change in her and, unlike everyone else, he's been demanding answers instead of making assumptions, but Rahab can't or won't explain herself. *Poor Sal, I wish I could tell him.* She is aware of how distant she's been. She runs faster.

Rahab and Salmone have played at the lake ever since she can remember. Salmone's father taught them how to fish there. Most Saturday mornings, Pastor Josh is on his boat with a line in the water while practicing his sermons. Rahab and Salmone are never too far behind him, pulling up crayfish cages.

Pastor Josh always jokes, "Catfish make the best congregation. Too bad we gonna eat'm afterward."

When Rahab reaches the lake, Salmone is packing to leave. She stops running and thrusts her hands on her knees, trying to catch her breath before walking over.

"Ah guess I'ma have to find me another fishing buddy," Salmone states, handing her her rod.

"Nothing biting?" Rahab asks, noticing his empty bucket. "Told ya my baits better." She smiles and nudges him.

They start to walk back towards the house as the sun begins to set.

"Ah used all ya bait setting de traps. You'll be here in de morning to help pull em up, right?"

"Yeah, I'll be here," Rahab answers, feeling she's let him down.

"De fish don't bite when I'm alone. Dey knows my heart ain't in it." He hangs his head.

"I'm sorry, Sal. Tings is just different right now," she tries to explain without explaining.

"Well, tings ain't never been different before, not 'tween us. We used to talk 'bout er'rything. No secrets, remember?" He reminds her of their friendship oath.

"Yeah but dis here is different. Ah just don't know how...ah..." Rahab stumbles for words as she chokes back tears.

Sensing something serious is bothering her, Salmone crosses over the muddy path to their favorite oak tree. He places his gear against the trunk and begins to climb. Rahab follows suit.

"You know, Rah, ah got secrets too." He looks at her over his shoulder, steadily climbing.

"No, you don't. You can't hold water."

"May! Ah do got me one. It's not lak a secret secret, just sumphin we don't talk 'bout much outside of de tree of us," he claims, referring to himself and his parents.

Salmone sits down on the edge of the deck that his father built for them. Rahab settles close. He breaks off a branch from the tree and starts pulling at the leaves.

"What is it, Sal?" Rahab asks, now curious. He looks sincere.

"Did ya know dat I'm adopted?"

Rahab's first reaction is to call him out on a lie, but she can tell by Salmone's fiddling that he's serious.

"What you mean adopted? Pastor Josh and First Lady ain't ya real ma and pa?" she asks, deciding to clarify the definition.

"Dey will always be my real Ma and Pa, fuh sho', but dey ain't have me like parents do."

"What? How dat be?" she asks, in 11-year-old confusion. "I've seen ya baby pictures, Sal, and First Lady always telling how you laugh lak ya Maw-Maw, real hearty like with ya head thrown back. And er'rybody knows you have ya pa's funny ways. Naw you saying you come from an orphanage, lak *Annie*?"

"No, stupid! Ah ain't say dat. Ah was a baby when dey got me, and it's easy to pick up someone's habits." He taps her over the head with the stick.

They briefly giggle then Salmone turns away and continues to pick leaves.

"Ah was born in El Paso, Texas. My biological father is Mexican, and my mother was a young Black woman," he informs, checking to see if Rahab is laughing. She isn't, she's observing him through new eyes.

Ooh, that's why those spiky hairs stick straight up on his head when his buzz cut is growing out. Rahab remembers asking Lotti about Salmone's funny hair. She laughingly said, "Dey must have Indian in der blood." Then she proceeded to remind Rahab that everyone's different and her own thick, golden sand colored hair is often the topic of conversation.

Feeling a tad bit self-conscious, Salmone continues his story. "My birth mother named me Salmone Demetrius," he reveals, checking again for laughter.

"Go on!" Rahab blurts, anxious to know his story.

"De year ah was born Ma and Pa were newly wedded missionaries in El Paso. Ma quickly became friends with a pregnant girl she met in de streets. De girl was hooked on drugs. One day she came to get sum food from de food truck de missionaries were sponsoring. She and Ma got to talking. She told Ma dat my father was either an illegal immigrant dat raped her when she was some place she wasn't supposed to be or a male friend who hung around de bar where she danced. Both men were Mexican," Salmone reveals, now doodling with the stick. He isn't quite sure Rahab understands but he continues anyway.

"Needless to say, Ma witnessed to her. Dat's sharing your sincere faith in Jesus Christ," he explains, knowing Rahab has no concept of Christian beliefs nor jargon.

He pauses briefly as a revelation floods his spirit. For the very first time, he knows in his heart why Rahab is in his life. *To save her like Ma and Pa saved me.* Salmone smiles and continues the rest of his story with pride.

89

"De young woman was repentant of her sins and wanted to be saved. She wanted to know de love of Jesus Christ. Ma took her in and in a few months, I'm born. De young woman, my birth mother, Carol, dies from a blood clot or sumphin de day after delivering me. Pa and Ma reach out to her family, but no one is willing to take in her bastard child. Dey tries to find de man from de bar, but no one owns up to her story or de name Demetrius. So, Pa and Ma head back to Orleans with a baby weaning from drugs. Dey re-name me Salmone Joshua Abrams. Pa, Ma, and Maw-Maw claimed me from day one as one of der own. Ma could never have babies. She says I'm God's gift to dem...special delivery. Dey told me lak it was, and ah don't keep it as no secret. It's our story, dat's all."

Rahab embraces Salmone's hand into hers and ceases his doodling. Tears are welling in his eyes. He pulls away from her and stands, pretending to stare off at the picturesque landscape. He quickly wipes his eyes.

"So, what you holding on to, huh? No secrets," Salmone demands, turning toward her.

Rahab buries her head between her knees, wrapping her arms around them and starts to cry.

Feeling responsible for her tears, Salmone comforts her. "What is it, Rah? I'll protect you. No matter what."

Salmone's declaration provokes her tears into a waterfall. She can't hold the secret back any longer. The unspoken day robbed her of enough time. *Maybe Sal will know if I'm pregnant or not. If I am, we can run away to New York together like my Ma.*

"Sal, ah. Well, you see...Doctor...Dr. Che–"

"Sal, Rah! Where y'at boy? Salmone, Rahab!" someone yells, interrupting.

90

Spontaneously, Salmone and Rahab look up at each other and then down the tree. Salmone's mother is yelling up at them from the base.

"Come down!" she requests. "Lotti's been taken to de hospital."

THE MESSAGE

Long, crossed, caramel colored legs embellished with fishnet stockings and red leather pumps sway nervously next to Rahab. Her red lips quiver and a white handkerchief dabs at the tears staining her painted face.

All she seems to do is cry. "Crying crocodile tears," Big Mama would say. Not once has she hugged me, smiled at me, or kissed me on the cheek. Not once has she said, "I'm sorry for your loss," as others have. Instead, she treats me like a ghost. Invisible.

From the moment Puah Marie Auguste stepped off the plane at New Orleans International airport, she has perfected the role of damsel-in-distress. She waltzed into town as the only mourning child of the deceased and fed on that title. No matter what happened between them, Charlotte *"Lotti"* Auguste was her mother.

Pride kept Puah tending to appearances, and all she offered Rahab was her handshake in an introduction. "I'm Puah," she said, extending a strong, straight and slender arm. Her wrist draped in gold. "I'm your mother. You may call me Pu, like everyone else."

She then ordered Rahab to follow her and stay out of the way.

The truth is, Lotti's death is an inconvenience to Puah. She's not ready to take on the responsibility of gaining another child. She's not yet willing to share her lifestyle with a daughter she doesn't know.

Charlotte Auguste was pronounced dead-on-arrival at St. Hope Hospital that somber Friday evening. The cause of death was a sudden cardiac arrest, but Rahab believes it was a broken heart. She never told her grandmother about the unspoken day but believed that the spirit of the ancestors revealed it to her.

Lotti was home alone that night with a Voodoo practitioner friend. According to the older woman they were involved in a possession ritual. She revealed to the family that Lotti solicited help from a Voodoo queen years ago. The favor had stipulations that Lotti ignored, and, her debt was due. Lotti never shared the details with the elder practitioner; she only mentioned its urgency. She was experiencing dark and sudden night visions. Visions that provoked her into worrying about Rahab's safety.

The older woman stated that she called on spirits to help reach the supreme creator. The *Loa*, a god in the Voodoo cult of Haiti, chose *to ride* (communicate through) the older woman. From that point, all the woman remembers is darkness and a feeling of flowing energy. She didn't recollect what the spirit imparted upon her nor what happened to Lotti. When she came through from the trance, she found Lotti folded over the table in a cold sweat, repeating softly, "Rahab, Rahab, Rahab."

Feeling weak herself, the senior practitioner assisted Lotti, but for Lotti, time was of the essence. She could feel the life being drained from her spirit. She begged the woman to listen. In her final breaths, she aimed to direct Rahab with the wisdom she thought she'd have time to teach. But time is no respecter of persons, and it waits for no one.

"Tell Rah I'm sorry. Tell her ah loves her. She's my heart. Tell her all she'll ever need to fight dis dark spirit and dis fallen world is in my metal box. Tell her to keep it close and use it. Don't be stubborn lak me, be better den me. Pass on de bol'in' pot."

The older woman, following orders, relayed the message to Rahab. Instead of saying metal box she said, "All you'll ever need is in her chest."

Rahab knew all about the chest containing gris-gris bags, potions, herbs, oils, and such. Everything she'll need to be just like her Big Mama.

J.C. MILLER

A RAINBOW IN THE SKY

I set my rainbow in the cloud, and it will be for a sign of a covenant between me and the earth.
Genesis 9:13

The House of Judah isn't as full as a Sunday morning. Instead, it seats a selected few. Since no one in Lotti's immediate family commits to organized religion, Puah and Mags opted to have a memorial instead of the traditional funeral or a Voodoo ritual for that matter. Pastor Josh offered to officiate over the service at his church and, unexpectedly, Puah and Mags accepted. Lotti spoke highly of him and his family, which was rare, so the offer seemed fitting.

Friends and acquaintances along the path of Lotti's life speak kindly of their time together. Mr. Brown, Lotti's *'lil boyfriend,* as she called him, addresses the assembly still intoxicated from a binge the night before.

"She was a woman hard to please and content in being left alone," he slurs, before suddenly breaking into tears. He can hardly compose himself. His honesty and drunken confessions are uncomfortable to hear. Given a few minutes more, Pastor Josh and Salmone usher him back to his seat. He stumbles down the aisle.

The Lawsons speak eloquently on behalf of the residents of *Money Mile.* From where Rahab sits, they seem to be the only ones from Money Mile in attendance. They offer Rahab a beautiful bouquet of flowers trimmed in lavender. The familiar scent brings tears to her eyes. The Lawsons, who operate in a sequence dance, bend over

Rahab so close that she can smell their morning coffee. Their bobbleheads touch as they wipe her cheeks, fix her hair into place and whisper condolences of inspiration. Somehow Puah acquires the flowers from Rahab and cries even more. Mags' rough dark hands draw Puah near as she pats her shoulder. Rahab picks up a fallen sprig of lavender from her lap and inhales it from a closed fist and smiles.

Big Mama would be pleased. She wouldn't want a fuss. I can hear her now saying, "That's wasted money."

Rahab looks around at all in attendance. She waves happily at Laura-Ann as their eyes meet in the mixed crowd. *Big Mama had more friends than she thought. She'd probably say, "They just here being nosey"*

Rahab closes her eyes, thinking of her beloved grandmother. Lotti stood for her own causes. She had no set religion, made no excuses, and always arranged her own time. Rahab can hear Lotti's voice preaching to her on her sad days, *"Time is precious, Rah. Never let anyone steal it from ya. We can't get it back."*

"Some would call Lotti a hard, selfish woman, but the truth is she loved with a hard hand. Good old-fashioned love."

Pastor Josh's vibrating voice bounces off the walls of The House of Judah, bringing Rahab back from the past. His accurate recognition of Lotti twirls around the rafters shakes the wooden floor planks and echoes in Rahab's heart.

"Charlotte *"Big Mama Lotti"* Auguste, although scorned by a hard life, found strength enough to take de lemons dat life threw her and made lemonade. Some mighty good lemonade." He laughs, causing the assembly's laughter. "Lotti was a businesswoman, an innovator ahead of her days, and my very dear friend. We bumped heads! We had us some heavy debates. In fact, some of you may already know dis, and some may find it as amazing as ah did, but Lotti knew de Bible to-and-fro," he states, flipping through the Bible forward and then backward. "I'm a tad bit ashamed to admit it, but she could recite chapters from memory better den ah can, and at de drop of a dime. Oh, she taught me some things, but we never could see eye-to-eye. We silently agreed to respect each other's callings with a nod of de head or a Big Mama Lotti hug. Naw dose was rare!" he jokes, causing laughter again.

"We did, however, have one agreement..." He strolls over to Rahab. "We agreed, as ah still do, dat dis 'lil angel is a gift from God. Charlotte loved her some Rahab. All her talk, and all her dreams, and all her work rested in her grandbaby. Yes, Lotti, we did agree on dat. Chile, ah still love ya," he declares, choking up. "My family and ah love ya, Rah, as if you were our own. Der is no distance, no family..." he emphasizes, looking over at Puah and Mags. "...dat can ever keep us away from you in spirit and in prayer."

He lifts Rahab's small body from her seat and carries her to the front of the altar.

"Please stand with me, church. Stretch ya hands toward Rah, de heart of her "Big Mama," Charlotte Auguste. Come into agreement with me as ah pray for a covering over dis here chile of God. Pray for her as she begins a new chapter in her life without de comfort of her maw-maw's arms."

Pastor Josh begins to pray and all of Lotti's friends and family come out from behind their pews, lifting their arms toward Rahab in a universal agreement. There is no separation of religion or color. Only the resounding sound of love expressed through prayer and moaning.

Pastor Josh, in a thunderous voice, intercedes on Rahab's behalf. He prays wholeheartedly for her well-being, comfort, wisdom, strength, and deliverance; that her path is made straight and her footsteps ordered by God. He squeezes Rahab tightly, unapologetically crying as he declares *the fruit of the Holy Spirit:* love, joy, peace, patience, kindness, goodness, faithfulness, gentleness, and self-control over her life in Jesus' name. Rahab wraps her arms around his neck in a loving embrace. He's the only father she's ever known. He hugs her back, oblivious to it being her last genuine hug from a man for many years to come.

Although they said this wasn't to be a religious service, the Holy Spirit didn't get the memo and enters the room as all in attendance give a resounding, "Amen." Rahab's balloon escapes it's imprisoning string and she doesn't feel like she's hovering above everyone else anymore. Beautiful colors seem to drift in twisting circles as her spirit enters back into its temple. At that moment, she understands that it's *God's love* that paints the sky.

There isn't a dry eye in *The House of Judah.* If it were possible to store a moment in time, Rahab would pick this one. Similar to a rainbow appearing after a good rain. Gazing upon the bow of bright colors stretched across the heavens, you believe. Then as the hues become misty and slowly vanish, you either remember its promise, forget it all together, or weep on soggy ground.

THE CONFIRMATION

Rahab's heart smiles at her rainbow as she scans the room with hope, until she locks eyes with evil. Her spirit is instantly cast to soggy ground. Dr. Chester lifts a finger to his thin puckered lips, and blows, "Shhh." He saunters through the crowd. Rahab's heart stops. She's deafened, and all she can see is him.

Salmone observes the fear in Rahab's eyes and follows her gaze in Dr. Chester's direction.

"Rah? Rah, you okay?" he questions, slightly yelling above the loud conversing around them.

Salmone pulls at Rahab's leg, but she doesn't move a muscle. Pastor Josh, who is still cradling her, mentally unwilling to hand her over to her selfish mother and foul-mouthed aunt, is speaking with the gathered group. When he finally acknowledges his sons pulling at Rahab's leg, he puts her down. She is noticeably trembling. Salmone grabs her hand and pulls her out of the church through the back door.

"You okay, Rah? What did he do?" Salmone queries, allowing his intuition to speak. Rahab strains her eyes against the bright sunlight. Salmone doesn't wait for an answer he leads her toward his bike. "Hop on! I'ma get ya outta here."

Before Rahab can think, she hops on the handlebars and they ride off. The wind quickly blows away her tears and her cheeks prickle with remorse.

Mama, why didn't I tell you? Now, what am I going to do? Pu doesn't want me, let alone a baby.

She wishes she could cry, but her voice seems lost in her throat.

Salmone turns his bike at the corner and heads out to the lake. Rahab wishes he would ride beyond the swamp, past the town, across the city limits, onto the highway, and away from Louisiana altogether. That's when an idea strikes her.

Before Salmone can come to a full stop, Rahab springs off of the bike and starts to climb *their tree* without speaking a word. Salmone scratches his head in wonderment. *She's acting like a girl and less like my buddy more and more every day.*

He starts to climb after her but notices she's wearing a dress and decides to wait until she reaches the deck. Whistling a song, he laughs inwardly at the glimpse he saw of her pink flowered *bloomers.*

Rahab's plan unravels with every sturdy branch she straddles.

"Wha'cha waiting on?" she yells down, anxious for him to arrive.

It doesn't matter what Dr. Chester did; she has a rainbow, Salmone, and, now, a plan.

She pulls Salmone's arms, helping him on to the landing. "Okay, I'm here...talk," he insists.

Rahab timidly steps away but then remembers her spirit came back. She lunges toward Salmone, almost knocking him off the deck.

"Coo, gal! What's wrong with ya?" he yells, regaining his footing then moving away from the edge of the deck.

Rahab pursues him, buzzing around like a mosquito hunting blood.

100

"Kiss me, Sal," she demands, trapping him in her arms. She puckers her lips and holds her head back with her eyes closed.

"Wait. What's going on? You gone fool, or sumphin?" Salmone asks, trying to escape her clutch.

"Kiss me, Sal. You need to kiss me. Don't you want to anyway?"

"No!" he lies, pulling away, embarrassed. *How did she know?* He moves out of Rahab's reach, but she's relentless. She begins to pull up her dress to take it off.

"Wait, stop! What are you doing?" he screams, pulling her dress back into place and fighting her off. "Rahab quit!" he finally demands.

"You don't understand, Sal," she cries.

Feeling defeated, Rahab flops down on the deck and begins to cry.

"Please explain." Salmone gets down on a knee near her.

"I'm pregnant!" Rahab blurts. "And ah want you to be de father, not him. We can run away together; please kiss me, Sal." She begins crying uncontrollably.

Salmone is flabbergasted. Lost in his thoughts, his mouth falls open. *What did she just say?*

"Rah, do you even know what you're talkin' 'bout?"

"Yes! Dr. Chester, he made me, he forced me to sit on his lap and he—"

"Stop!" Salmone yells, covering his ears.

He stands and turns away. He wasn't expecting this type of secret. Fear and anger crowd him. *How could I have let this happen?* He automatically assumes responsibility for the worst kind of intrusion. *All this time I thought she found another friend or something.* He silently attempts to work out his feelings.

"What...did...he...do...toyou?" Salmone emphasizes, walking back toward her.

His face is red. His fists are balled up. His eyes are watery. Rahab jumps up, unfamiliar with this side of him.

"Tawk, Rahab Auguste, dis is serious." Salmone grabs her arms. "People go to jail for stuff lak dis!"

Rahab hadn't considered that. *Have I broken the law?*

"Ah don't wanna go to jail, he tricked me! He said he wants a kid lak me," she cries.

"What did he do, Rah?" Sal asks calmly but afraid to his core.

"He touched me, he rubbed my legs and all o'va. He pulled at my clothes, kissin' and lickin' my face and neck. He was pantin' and breathin' hot air on my ears. He...he touched my private parts. Grabbed me real hard and..." She buries her face in Salmone's chest, ashamed. "Help me, Sal. Ah don't wanna be pregnant."

"What else? Did he do anything else?" Salmone asks, holding her and crying himself. *Was she raped like my mother?* He clasps his heart. It's rapidly pumping like it's going to explode from his chest. "Did he...did he rape you?" he finally asks.

Rahab looks up at him in confusion, her eyes are red and swollen from crying. Salmone isn't sure how to rephrase the question or if he should be asking at all. He needs to know.

"Rah, did he pluck ya flower?" He awkwardly manages to ask in spite of embarrassment. He examines

102

her face for understanding and sees none. "Did he put his private part in your private part?"

"NO!" Rahab yells, pulling away in disgust. "No! Sal, dat's disgusting. Dogs do dat. Why would he do dat?"

"Dat's...dat's how you get pregnant. Animals, people...they do dat with their mates. Dey make love and make babies. Big Mama ain't never told you 'bout de birds and de bees? You ain't hear it in school?"

"What?" Rahab yells in confusion. "First der's tadpoles and goat heads, naw birds and bees. Big Mama told me never let boys touch my treasure box or I'll get pregnant. Dat's it!"

No wonder why no one told me where babies come from, they were too ashamed. Rahab remembers Laura-Ann's laughter, Ms. Ruby's choking, and Big Mama flipping through the pages of *Gray's Anatomy.* "No wonder," she whispers, flopping down on the deck.

Salmone sighs in relief but he's still hot with anger so he begins to pace. He's never felt this way before.

How dare Dr. Chester.

"Rah is my girl," he mutters, punching his fist into his hand. Then freezes, realizing his spoken declaration. He turns to see if she heard him.

"Rahab is your wife," an audible voice speaks.

Salmone looks up toward the sky and closes his eyes. He's heard the Lord speak to him before. When he battled with feelings of inadequacy and questions regarding his birth parents, God spoke to him saying, **"This is your real mother, and this is your real father. You are a part of them."** Being a firm believer, that was all Salmone needed then and God's word is all he needs now.

103

"Lord, is she?" he whispers in astonishment. Not doubting but confirming. *Should I know this so young in life?*

Salmone glances at Rahab, her eyes are red and swollen, but she's still the prettiest girl he knows.

There's nothing she cannot do when she puts her mind to it. Salmone smiles at her plans to run away with him. Now she looks like the world is on her shoulders. His heart breaks. She'll be leaving for New York soon. She'll be making new friends and making new boys laugh and fall in love with her. I don't know how You plan on making her my wife one day, Lord, but until then I better tell her all there is to know about things. Salmone walks over and sits down beside her.

"Rah, I'm sorry 'bout er'rything. Ah wish you would have told me sooner. We have to let de grown-ups know what hap—"

"No, Sal! Ah can't," Rahab whines, cutting him off.

Salmone places his arm around her shoulders and draws her near. "Listen, we got to tell. What dat cooyon did is wrong, and he'll keep doing it to other girls if we don't stop him."

"I'm ashamed, ah can't."

"I'ma tell fuh ya. I'll protect you too," he states, holding his chest out a little higher.

Rahab rests her head on his shoulder. *He's right.* She doesn't want Dr. Chester to hurt anyone else but, at the moment, the joy of not being pregnant is all she can manage to handle.

"You're moving to New York soon. It's time someone explains tings to ya," Salmone relates, worried that she's too naive.

"Please do and tell me de truth."

Salmone remembers his father praying for Rahab's safety, and without filters, he informs her with all he knows. He proceeds to gently describe the human reproductive system just as his father explained to him. He talks about God's intentions for the marriage union and how man hasn't always upheld to that plan. He speaks of the consequences of our actions in both the spiritual and physical realm and God's forgiving love. The more he shares, the more he realizes how much he loves her. Beyond friendship, his pure love explodes.

Until my love brings her back, at least she'll be wise.

Salmone and Rahab sit hand-in-hand in silence allowing awareness to sink in. From the deck, the stretch of the lake becomes smaller in comparison to the world they must face. The remaining pieces of their childhood shed away. Salmone prays in his heart for her and the Holy Spirit confirms, **"Rahab, is your wife."**

REVEALED

He reveals the deep and secret things; he knows what is in the darkness, and the light dwells with him.
Daniel 2:22

When Salmone and Rahab returned to the church from the lake, all the guests had already left. The Abrams family, along with Puah and Mags, were sitting at a table quietly talking. Their bellies were full of the donated dishes the congregation supplied for the repast. Their empty plates sat in front of them as they sipped on hot coffee. Ms. Simmons, one of the church's elders, stayed behind to tidy up, hum, and pray. Mr. *Lil Boyfriend* Brown sat in the corner with his back leaning against the wall, fast asleep. Salmone and Rahab quietly entered, dripping the water from a few fish they caught behind them.

"Ooh, der dey go! Nice of y'all to join us," Pastor Josh complained loudly above all the other complaints.

"Sal, ah done told ya 'bout dem fish, you messin' up mi floors. You gone pass de mop fuh sho, boy," Ms. Simmons argued, taking the fish from him. She hurried toward the kitchen mumbling under her breath.

"Pa, ah got sumpin' important to say," Salmone boldly declared, ignoring the complaints. Rahab stood hiding behind him with her head held low.

"It better be important, y'all been missing for nearly two hours. People wanted to give Rah—"

"What is it, chile?" Ms. Ruby interrupted, noticing her grandson's nervous fidgeting and his hidden friend. "Come here," she added, extending her hands.

106

Salmone moved forward, taking his grandmother's hands. Rahab followed in his steps.

"Maw-Maw, Dr. Chester done hurt Rah," he blurted.

Suddenly, all of the chatting and laughter stopped.

"What de hell did you say?" Mags demanded, sitting straight in her seat.

Knowing her aunt's type of person, Puah firmly gripped Mags' shoulder reminding her of her whereabouts.

"Let de boy speak," Pastor Josh suggested, pulling his son toward himself. He quickly searched Rahab's eyes and found heart-wrenching sadness. "What do you mean by hurt, Junya?" he asked calmly, already praying in his spirit.

"He hurt her, Pa. Invaded her personal space like you done told me a man shouldn't."

Feeling ashamed, Rahab wrapped her arms around Salmone's waist and hid her face into his back, crying.

Mags, the fighter of the family, moved to the edge of her seat. Her legs were agape inappropriately for a woman in a dress and her hands pushed down on each knee. If need be, she was ready to leap up and fight.

"I'm ten seconds away from getting arrested in this son-of-a-beeswax," she warned calmly, yet very serious. Her eyes blinked and rolled with every word. "Make ya'self crystal clear, Junya," she mocked.

Salmone started to get nervous, but Rahab squeezed harder and brought his courage back. "He took her down to de lake, made her sit on his lap and touched and kissed on—"

"Oh, hell nah!" Mags interrupted, springing up and heading for the door.

In shock, Puah had released her grip on Mags' shoulder. Her eyes now rested on her daughter's. They were sad and innocent.

"RAHAB!" Puah sang, in a screeching tune.

Before then, Puah couldn't figure out how to begin the healing process of mending their estranged relationship. However, her motherly instinct naturally kicked in upon hearing Rahab's dreadful fate. In a moment's time, Rahab advanced from estranged to beloved. Puah's love for her grew more in that *twinkling* than in her lifetime.

Puah scooped her trembling daughter into her arms and allowed her to do the crying for a change. She closed her eyes and pressed her lips tightly together, inwardly weeping. She didn't realize she could suddenly feel so strongly for the abandoned child. Maybe she always did? She was sorry but sorry was hardly enough. She cupped Rahab's head against her shoulder and paced the room in nervous energy. She became deaf to everything but the howling sound of her daughter's haunting cry.

Salmone continued Rahab's story as heads dropped in sadness. Mags listened by the door with her foot blocking Ms. Simmons' reentrance with the mop. She ignored the woman's gesturing through the vertical window pane on the door to let her in.

"We gotta call de police," someone finally said. "He can't get away with dis."

Puah did not agree with what everyone else in the room thought was a good idea. "NO!" She yelled, ending her pacing. "My child has been through enough, I'm—"

"You can't be serious?" Pastor Josh interjected.

Mags quietly exited the room, on the hunt for a dead man. She warned Ms. Simmons to stay out while the family talked privately.

"I'm taking my daughter home, Pastor," Puah finished.

"We can't just allow him to mess with our children and walk free," Pastor Josh countered, walking toward her.

"NO!" Puah yelled, turning Rahab away from him in protection. "We are going home to New York City. Away from this blood sucking swamp. I don't care what you do, but Rahab will no longer be subject to this suffering. It ends here," Puah insists, remembering her past.

It felt right to protect Rahab. It seemed right to Puah to do what she does best, run.

"But Pu—"

"Joshua," First Lady calmly interjected, resting her hand on the Pastor's shoulder. She began rubbing her husband's back, then added. "She said her peace, let her tink on it. Maybe, she'll feel differently tomorrow? Let's all go on home and tink dis ting o'va."

"We won't be here in the morning," Puah stated, standing her ground.

"God's speed," First Lady bade, nodding her head.

Pastor Josh attempted to interject but his wife put a finger over his mouth.

THE WOODEN CHEST

Puah and Mags sit comfortably in their reserved *Amtrak* seats with their feet resting on the bench seat facing them. Rahab lays sprawled across their laps asleep. Their trip to New York City was delayed another day because, at the last minute, Rahab refused to board the plane with Puah and Mags.

They felt she'd been through enough and didn't press the issue. They settled on staying overnight in town and the next morning they boarded a twenty-nine-hour trip to New York City.

By taking the train, they were able to travel with Lotti's wooden chest. Rahab insisted upon not leaving Louisiana without it. The Abrams family agreed to hold Lotti's boiling pot until arrangements could be made to pick it up from them. But her chest rides securely alongside Rahab.

Besides family history and plenty of memories, the cumbersome wooden chest contains old pictures, letters, Lotti's sterilized medical tools wrapped in cheesecloth, bags of dried herbs, small labeled bottles of elixirs, a book of remedies, jars of corn liquor, and a small metal lock-box. The same metal box Lotti hid under the floorboards when she was younger. Inside of the box were vital records, Lotti's Bible, deeds, and a bank book. Lotti safeguarded money for Rahab just as she had done for Puah when she was younger. This time she added a security clause stating said monies were only to be withdrawn by Rahab upon her twenty-fifth birthday. The stipulation was added to keep Puah away from it.

J.C. MILLER

A HEAVY CONSCIENCE

As the train rumbles on, the vast lakes and farmland of the south give way to northern complexity and allow Puah a window pane view of the intricacy of her complicated life.

Rahab's heavy head rests against Mags' bosom like a sack of rocks. Puah smiles at the thought of wishing she could rest her head on her Tante Mags' breast again as she did as a child. *That was some of the best sleep.* She remembers, now examining Rahab's angelic sleeping face.

She's undeniably handsome.

When Puah left home, Rahab was still an infant. Her eyes barely opened. Now they're a fascinating hazel color shifting between green, blue, and gray. She was bald then; now her hair, hidden underneath Salmone's baseball cap, is like a desert of golden sand. Puah lifts Rahab's small foot lying in her lap and rubs it. She doesn't move an inch.

"Poor thing, she's exhausted," Puah whispers, now studying her daughter's toes. Miniature versions of her own.

In Rahab's presence, Puah feels ashamed, awkwardly naked as if under a telescope. Being herself isn't good enough. She can't help but appear a blubbering mess. She knows that she can be selfish at times, more times than maybe a mother should. Her selfishness, often misconstrued as her character, is a survival technique. It wasn't her intention to ignore Rahab; it just happened that way.

Puah closes her eyes to keep from tearing. *I missed her growing up.* She broods over kissing baby feet and

111

nuzzling a chubby milk-scented neck. Not able to keep her tear filled eyes off of Rahab, Puah observes her already substantially developed breasts and realizes her baby is nearly a teen now and shapelier than she recalls herself at eleven. *It's no wonder Mama kept her dressed like a boy.*

"Tsk, few more months and she's got me."

I wonder who's taller, she or Si? Puah thinks of her only son who's recently turned eleven. She sighs at the thought of introducing the siblings and explaining how a mother could abandon her child for nearly twelve years.

Puah finally slips into sleep with a heavy conscience and an even heavier heart. The trip back to Louisiana, although a sad occasion, was good for both she and Mags. At least until Rahab's news. Puah was thrown back into her reality of abandonment while Mags fought off the voices of some demons of her own.

THE HAND HE DEALT

Mags ventured out to find Dr. Chester that night, seeking to deal him the hand he dealt Rahab. She wanted him to die in the misery of losing hope, the fear of being taken advantage of, and the torment of having no power. Before heading to Dr. Chester's house, she stopped in a bar and downed a few shots of corn liquor. An alcoholic, Mags hadn't drank since leaving New York City.

"Do it for Charlotte," voices echoed in her mind. "She fought your battles," they incited.

Mags crouched behind the bushes in the good doctor's backyard. Her heart raced as she slipped a razor underneath her tongue. She tried to straighten her back, but the years that crept upon her were apparent.

"I'll do it hunched over," she whispered, peeking around a bush.

The house seemed quiet. She figured she'd make her entrance through the basement door then up to the doctor's room. She learned he had a night maid from the men in the bar and hoped their paths wouldn't cross. She intended on taking only one life. Her detailed plan required slipping into Dr. Chester's room and straddling him in his sleep. Then covering his mouth and nose until his face turned purple and his eye bulged. Right before dying she'd push his forehead back, revealing his vulnerable neck, then spit the razor out like a snake and slice him across the windpipe. She'd laugh and watch him gurgle and drown in his own blood.

Before taking the deep step into insanity, Mags smelled smoke. She peeked from her hiding place and noticed a blaze of fire coming from the front yard. It lit the darkened sky. Her plans were foiled. Before retreating, she peeked again. Salmone was running across the backyard toward the hedges.

"Well do Lord! As I live and breathe," she whispered in shock.

"Psst!" Mags sounded as loud as she could, standing out in the open and gesturing him over. *He beat me to it.* She smiled, moving back behind the bushes. *He's burning the house down.* At that moment, she kindled a liking toward him.

She grabbed him as he ran by, pulling him through the thick hedges. They didn't have time to talk. They ran through the woods that paralleled *Money Mile* as fast as they could. Salmone led the way. He was looking for a patch of wild fern nestled between two walnut trees. The spot where he laid his bike. Mags struggled to keep up. She had to abandon her pumps to move quicker. When he stopped to retrieve his bike, she grabbed him by the arm and forced him to stand still for a moment while she caught her breath.

"You don't ever have to tell, ya hear?" she managed to say, breathing heavily. Her body drenched in sweat. Salmone began to cry. He'd never done anything like that. Mags hugged him. "Hush now, it's okay."

"Ah set fire to his garden," he admitted, sobbing.

"What? That's it?" Mags yelled, pushing him away. "That's all you did?" She wanted Dr. Chester dead - burned to death in his sleep.

"He scared Rah in dat garden," Salmone cried. "He treasured it lak a baby, pruning and such, den he stole her innocence. Ah just wanted to take sumphin from him

114

dat he loved. Sumphin he would never see again. He'll never see dat same rose garden ever again!" Salmone wiped away tears. "Dat's all ah could do."

Mags drew him in again and hugged him tightly. "You don't ever have to tell, ya hear? No one has to know."

No one knew but Dr. Chester. He watched from the windows of his dreary room. He started to yell when he saw Salmone pouring gasoline around the perimeter of his maze garden. But he recognized him as Rahab's friend. Righteousness seized his vocal cords. Tears leaked from his eyes as he stood sobbing at the window, his hands gripping the frame. He watched in torment as his beloved garden grew engulfed in flames. *Poetic justice.* Salmone stood in a victorious stance. His imaginary red cape fluttered in the gentle night breeze. Dr. Chester watched the boy, more honorable than he, run out of the yard and disappear behind the hedges. The loss stabbed like a knife. *All those years of careful planning, trimming, fertilizing, and pruning all gone.* But what he did to Rahab would forever be etched upon the timeline of her life

Dr. Chester thought he'd stopped luring little girls; he hadn't done it since his hospital years. But there was something about Rahab, an enticement he couldn't avoid. He instantly lusted after her. He didn't deserve beautiful roses. He allowed the garden to burn and vowed never to replace it.

A few weeks later, Dr. Chester was found by the lake not far from the spot where he stole Rahab's spirit. After discovering he'd been reported to child welfare services, he decided his own fate and died a miserable coward.

NEW YORK CITY

BIG EASY TO BIG APPLE

"New-awlins is sho nuff hot but dis here hot is lak a brick oven!" Rahab loudly proclaims over the rumbling of the city. She scrunches her face and fans herself with Salmone's cap. The heat, emerging from the tunnels below, consumes her with no relief of a shady tree. The ravaging conditions don't seem to bother the flood of people monopolizing the sidewalks. They only make it hotter.

Rahab has never witnessed so many people chaotically massed together in one place before. Protected under Puah's watchful eyes, she stands fascinated yet slightly frightened by how insignificant she feels amongst the immensity of the notorious realm of*The Big Apple.*

Her mind swells with questions. *Where will I live? How will I make friends? There're so many people! I hope I don't get lost.* Anxiety creeps up on her, but Puah's constant reassurance and a firm grip on her shoulder re-establish safety. Rahab circles her mother in wonderment. Awe-stricken, she gazes up at the tall buildings. The skyscrapers seem to tilt or sway against the late afternoon sky. The superstructures climb up and down across the city setting, mimicking giant building blocks. They glow in bright lights, mirrored windows, and brilliant billboards.

It's a hot, early September, late afternoon. Mags, Puah, and Rahab are standing in front of *Penn Station* waiting for Richard to arrive. People carelessly rush by, bumping into them without apologies, and every so often someone knocks over a piece of luggage and Mags delivers them a few choice words. To Rahab, the growing crowd appears stylish and well put together. Admiring them, she feels raggedy and underdressed. Her cut-off overalls, faded orange *Houston Astros* tee-shirt, and canvas sneakers had seen their last days months ago.

After keeping the trio waiting in the scorching heat, Richard W. Owens finally arrives. He casually pulls up twenty minutes late, driving a fancy burgundy colored *1981 Lincoln Mark VI* trimmed in silver and gold. The interior is draped in creamy white leather. White wall tires with gold and silver rims complete the pimped-out ride.

Rahab has never seen a car so dolled-up before. Lotti's patrons on *Money Mile* drive nice cars but none as fancy as Mags and Richard's. *They must be filthy rich.* She can't wait to get in and fidget around.

Richard, dressed in the same creamy color as the car's interior, steps out attracting plenty of attention of his own. His hair, black and lightly salted, is smooth and wavy against his head. His light textured pants sway with his movements, and the gold medallion hanging from his neck sparkles against the city lights. As he turns the corner of his car, his cream-colored alligator shoes seem to growl at Rahab. If Richard had theme music, it would be *Curtis Mayfield's* "Superfly."

"So, this is her?" Richard asks, smiling and revealing a gold eye tooth and dimples that match Rahab's. He removes his *Ray-Ban Wayfarer* shades to examine her. In a smooth yet profound sing-a-song tone of voice, he proclaims, "She's a keeper." With a nod of approval toward Mags and Puah, he stoops low and surveys Rahab's face. His breath smells of peppermint. "Oh snap, she looks exactly like my Ma Mabel. God rest her soul," Richard exclaims, shocked by Rahab's resemblance to his mother. He lifts her off her feet so that they're eye to eye. Even against Lotti's despise for him, Rahab can't help but smile. Richard is still charming, and he smells of holiday spices. "Same color hair and everything. I can remember Ma Mabel brushing that pretty hair every night before bed. I use to fall asleep watching her do that. And look at these beautiful eyes. Practically twins," he adds, now feeling sentimental. He twirls Rahab around in the air to keep himself from tearing up. He hasn't thought of his mother since he was a boy fighting to forget her.

Ma Mabel was a tiny mulatto woman from South Carolina. She moved to New York to pursue a singing career and escape the many prejudices within her own community. She could pass for white, better than a white woman could. The city treated her fairly. Ma Mabel was able to create a new life for herself. By and by, she met and fell in love with a sweet-talking Sicilian. He owned a nightclub and promised her the moon and stars, but her secret caught up with her. Discovering she was a Negro woman, the love of her life severely beat her and left her for dead. She survived the beating with a limp, a deep scar above her right eye, and a handsome baby boy. To keep a roof over their heads and food on the table, she struggled as a seamstress by day and a hooker by night. Ma Mabel died suddenly of pneumonia at the tender age of twenty-nine, Richard was just eight-years-old. He spent the remainder of his childhood in and out of foster homes and juvenile detention centers. One day, sleeping on the streets of Harlem, he met a man with a saxophone who took him under his wing.

Richard's eyes glisten with held back tears. Ma Mabel's image had faded until Rahab. He smiles at the notion of one person cloning another and the possibilities of giving Rahab the life his mother never had. Mags and Puah enclose them with a hug.

CHARLOTTE STREET

The excitement of being in the city quickly turns into fear of death on the highway. New York City traffic makes the ride to Puah's house seem as long as the trip from New Orleans. Richard quickly darts his *Lincoln* into any free space on the highway, then dares fellow motorists to hit his baby. Angry commuters honk their horns and try to gain access to Richard's side view. He and Mags, the tag team duo, yell profanities through their opened windows and bang on the outside of the car doors, daring drivers to approach the vehicle. Afraid, Rahab curls up under Puah's arm.

"Stop, Richard. You're scaring my baby," Puah laughingly announces over the loud sounds of traffic.

Richard and Mags roll up their windows. Enthralled in road rage, they forgot they had passengers.

"Jive turkeys. Ain't no need for worry, Tante Maw-Maw don't play. I jumps frog," Mags voices, extending her palm for Puah to slap her a five.

The cityfied trio then commences in adult conversation so vulgar that Rahab covers her own ears.

Finally, they reach Puah's house. *Wow.* Rahab gawks suspiciously at her new surroundings. *If the car ride didn't kill me, this neighborhood will.* Blinded by the *bright lights of the big city* she'd forgotten about the crime reports she and Lotti used to watch on *WDSU News 6.* Lotti used to shake her head and suck her teeth saying, "Ah don't know why Puah Marie would want to live in dat dangerous city. Ah swear dat gal don't use de brains de almighty done gave her."

121

Is this a pit stop? Rahab hopes. Her heart confirms differently. Richard stopped in front of a small teal colored, prefabricated, ranch-style home with black shingles. Leading up the neatly cut hedge-lined walkway and toward the barred front door, Minton sits in a lawn chair on a small paved porch. Just getting in from work, he was enjoying a cigar when they pulled up. With licked callused fingertips, he swiftly puts out the stogie then tucks it behind his ear and struts down the walkway. He swings open Puah's door. A Cheshire Cat smile showing bright teeth spreads across his face as if to say, *"Come to Poppa."* He licks his lips, clapping and rubbing his hands together.

Puah steps out and throws her arms in the air yelling, "My baby."

"Uh huh," Minton responds, taking her into his strong arms. "I bet you had a good time catching up with dem good ole boys," he jealously adds, kissing and hugging her like they haven't seen each other in years.

Minton glimpses at Rahab sitting in the back seat and makes no acknowledgments. She's slightly intimidated by him. He's dressed in a navy blue Dirty South Dry Cleaning uniform. His huge muscles seem too big for the short-sleeved outfit. He isn't what Rahab imagined for Puah, neither suave nor debonair. He's rugged like most bayou men. *By the looks of this neighborhood, he's definitely needed.* Rahab tries not to stare.

"Hey, save that mess for later," Richard yells, getting out and walking toward Minton. "Check out my beautiful grandbaby."

The men exchange a manly handshake routine ending in an armed hug.

122

"Yeah man, I see her. She cute like my bay-bee over here," Minton jokes, squeezing Puah a little harder. She stares proudly between him and Rahab trying to figure their thoughts. Minton's smile fades as he rubs his goatee like a man in deep thought. That slightly worries Puah.

"Yo, help me with all this luggage ya woman packed," Richard requests, opening the trunk. "I finally got one that looks like me, bro," he adds, still bragging about Rahab as he hands Minton a bag.

"I'm still waiting on one to look like me," Minton jokes.

He and Puah's kids are a beautiful mixture between his milk chocolate skin and her caramel complexion. Silas is all legs, athletic and handsome. At eleven, Puah is already beating girls off with a stick. Gomer is Puah's chunky princess. She's an eight-year-old with attitude and has the house wrapped around her pinky finger. She reminds Puah of Lotti with her bushy shoulder length hair, rosy cheeks, and brown chestnut shaped eyes.

"What the heck is that?" Minton queries, noticing Lotti's chest in the trunk.

"Don't ask, bruh," Richard laughingly advises. "You don't wanna know."

"It ain't none of that Voodoo crap, is it? Because I—"

"It's just a few of mama's memories, that's all," Puah answers, cutting him off. She doesn't want him and Mags arguing today.

Mags knows that Puah and Minton's relationship isn't what it used to be, and she tries to hold her tongue out of respect.

"I remember this chest from my apartment on North Rampart. Mama Lotti had some sweet-smelling stuff in there. I think she added it to the steam water at my cleaners. Had the customers requesting it for weeks after y'all left. You know how to make that stuff, Pu?" Minton rambles, not noticing the tears collecting in the eyes of those that Lotti loved.

"Yeah man, I remember that smell," Richard relates, reminiscing. "She was the sweetest smelling girl I ever met...and that stuff was lethal! She used to take that oil and rub it all over...had a brother like...ya know?" he whispers, acknowledging Mags in the front seat.

"I can still hear you, Richard," Mags retorts, tilting her head slightly. "Ain't nobody gonna be talking about my sister out the side of they mouth. And ain't nobody gonna be messing with her poppycock either."

"Yes, ma'am, Tante Mags, no disrespect," Minton answers, knocking elbows and winking eyes with Richard.

Before Puah can open the front door, two overly excited kids meet her *oohing and ahhing* over Lotti's chest.

"Pu is that for me?" Gomer asks, dancing and sucking a lollipop.

"No, dummy, it's for me. Right, Pu?" The eldest corrects her, hugging Puah around the waist.

Puah laughs nervously, quickly glancing back at Rahab. She's sitting in the car, peeking through the window. Puah requested earlier that she have some time alone with the kids before introductions. She needed to explain why Rahab was coming to live with them.

Mags admiringly smiles from the car, watching as Silas and Gomer jump all over Paw-Paw as they call Richard. He treats each child with tenderness, pulling magic quarters from behind their ears and gives them money and peppermints. Mags loves him dearly, but she trusts him about as far as she can throw him. Richard loves Mags right back. He can't help his roaming eyes nor Mags her itchy trigger finger. They try not to bump heads on that issue, but if you're a female and walking, Richard's looking, no matter the relation.

Having him around my girls is going to get tough, especially with Miss Shapely over here. Mags glances back at Rahab from the rearview mirror. She reminded her of herself when she was younger. *I don't care how much he thinks she looks like his so-called Ma Mabel. He's a lie and a cheat, and I'll kill him over my girls.* She turns around in her seat and looks at Rahab, assessing her as innocent as well as noticeably nervous.

"I sho am glad to have all you kids around," Mags finally states, trying to redirect her attention. "Y'all give me and Paw-Paw a new hand at life. I wasn't able to have no babies myself..." she continues, staring past Richard and the kids and off into another place and time. "...but life sho' is funny. Now we have three grandbabies, ain't that something?"

"Yup, everything's gonna be alright," Richard expresses, getting back in the car. He notices Rahab's uncertain demeanor. "Things are just as they should be." He smiles devilishly at Mags. He's aware that she's vexed over his earlier remark about Lotti. He leans in and pecks her on the cheek, then playfully slaps her thigh. She giggles girlishly.

"It sho is."

WINDOW VIEW

Rahab sinks low into the leather bench seat of her fancy ride. She peeks through the lightly tinted windows, wondering if there are any rivaling street gangs in the area. Her stomach bubbles with nervous jitters as they drive away from her new home. Richard planned an early seafood dinner on City Island while the Williams family talked things through.

This isn't the lifestyle I expected.

Rahab tries to imagine Puah with her beautiful dresses, gold jewelry, and long red painted nails, walking the streets of such a place. *There must be some mistake.* She fancied Puah living in a penthouse like *The Jeffersons* on television. *These people aren't anything like the ones from earlier. Limos aren't a dime a dozen here.*

Rahab notices the kids playing in the streets and observes they aren't much different from those she left behind in the river parish. The young boys, playing stickball in the street, ignore angry drivers trying to pass. The drivers honk their horns and yell obscenities. Only after completing a swing do the boys scatter to bordering sidewalks. Unlike the lads of the bayou, these young men lift double middle fingers and grab their tiny crotches as the angry motorists drive by. Rahab clinches the amulet around her neck. Sassy little girls jump *double dutch* and sing familiar schoolyard chants. Only they add R-rated verses and whining bodies to their songs. *No "Abba Daba Honeymoon" here*

More familiar are the women walking to and fro pushing babies or shopping carts full of grocery or laundry

126

bags. Mothers yell through open windows at any child acting up. Teenagers sit on the stoops listening to loud music, playing cards, and *dishing the dozens.* Considering the time of day, Rahab figures the men are probably stuck in traffic coming home from work. The few she can find are either playing dominoes, bouncing basketballs, or holding up a wall with their arched backs staring into space. Everyone seems to possess an aura of street confidence. They appear to be hardened and distant. No passers-by with smiling eyes hoot hearty greetings with hugs or kisses. Everyone seems satisfied within their individual squares amongst the sidewalk.

How will I survive? Why did Big Mama have to die?

The reality of life and the responsibility of living makes itself evident. When Lotti was alive, Rahab didn't have to worry about what she ate, where to sleep, or was she safe; that was a given luxury. The assurance of her new family's reliability hasn't set in.

As Rahab stares at the two strangers known as her grandparents catching up on business, she experiences a moment of vivification. An unscheduled rebirthing. *It's time for me to grow up. It's time to put to practice all of the lessons Big Mama taught.* She takes her place in life, mentally *cutting the apron strings.* Tears flood her eyes as she slumps deeper into her seat and squeezes her amulet tighter. *I guess Charlotte Street is an okay place for new beginnings.* She comforts herself, comparing her new home to the surrounding areas Richard is driving through.

Charlotte Street, once declared a symbol of urban decay, is a diamond in the rough. It's three blocks of newly constructed, cookie cutter, gated ranch-style homes. Treeling lined sidewalks introduce the small manicured lawns of the hard-working family homes. Turning the corner off of Charlotte sits Silas and Gomer's elementary school. The historic architectural gothic designed school is gated to keep hoodlums off the property. On every block is a Cuchifritos, Chinese, Soul, or fast food restaurant contending for the overweight natives' money. Liquor stores near every church rival for the rest.

Mags points out that Crotona Park isn't far from Rahab's new abode. "...buying candy won't be a problem with a bodega on every corner," she informs.

Completing the surrounding neighborhoods are weed-choked vandalized lots, project buildings, and old tenements decorated in graffiti and boarded windows. Flame burnt cars sit abandoned along the streets. *Can these people truly be happy?* Rahab wonders, watching smiling faces go about living. *Maybe this is one of those 'don't judge a book by its cover' lessons Big Mama used to preach.* She dries her eyes with the back of her hands and sits straight, content with the possibility of things looking worse than they really are. *How else, besides having a personal security guard, would Puah have made it all of these years?* She edges closer to the window and discovers people venturing from their squares upon the sidewalk, and living, in spite of their circumstances.

I'll have to become a woman to survive.

IRISH TWINS

At first, Silas and Gomer were shy and standoffish. Silas, acquainted with being the older sibling, didn't fancy handing over his title. When Puah revealed having and hiding another child and why they cried as though they'd lost a loved one. Gomer mostly cried because Silas did. Secretly she entertained the idea of gaining a sister. Silas, knowing all about sex and where babies come from, cried because his mother was abused and raped. Naturally, he was also upset that Puah would abandon a child and then hide her from them. The security of parental trustworthiness disintegrates as he wondered what else she's hiding. *Are we safe?* As it was, Silas and Gomer spent far too much time home alone or with their grandparents.

Feeling awkward beside Rahab, Silas can't deny his new sister is oddly attractive. They stand back to back as Puah measures them against each other. Rahab stands tall and straight, knowing she's short for her age, but Silas still measures two inches over her.

"Irish twins," Puah declares, being that Silas recently turned eleven and Rahab turns twelve in a few days.

"You sure she's older than me?" Silas gloats satisfied with at least being taller if not older.

Rahab, who usually challenges boys who make her feel inadequate, surrenders under his taunting. She desperately needs a friend, and he's her only chance of making it in the hood. *A brother to depend on, like Sal.* The thought of Salmone brings a lump to her throat. She

129

closes her eyes, allowing the feeling to pass. The last thing she wants is to come across as a crybaby in front of her new brother. From what little she can tell, he's nothing like Salmone. He's overconfident, whereas Salmone is humble. Silas appears graceful, whereas Salmone is known to trip over his own feet. Silas lacks the mannerism of a gentleman, whereas Salmone is gallant. Silas is just like every boy she's fought to gain respect. The only difference is he's her brother, and she needs to befriend him.

Silas knows everyone, and everyone knows him. He maneuvers through the harsh city blocks on his bike like his grandfather in the *Lincoln*. It doesn't take Rahab long to fit in amongst her siblings. It turns out they need her as much as she needs them.

HOUSE OF PAIN

Although grateful for the blessing of Rahab's love, Puah isn't the mother she promised to be. Instead of nurturing her kids, she elects to cater to Minton and drinks more than a mother should. She works nights at the hospital and sleeps during the day. On her downtime, she and Mags *shop until they drop. Macy's, Gimbels, Bloomingdales, Tiffany,* and *B. Altman* love to see the Auguste women coming through the doors.

Puah's motto is, "A family falling apart, doesn't have to look the part."

"You pick up where I slack off, and this extended family might work out," she explains to Rahab, requiring more and more of her. "Work for me, and I'll work for you," Puah justifies, lavishing her with gifts.

Rahab doesn't mind the hard work. She'd do it even if there were no gifts involved. The family is all she has. Fitting in, both in and outside of the home, was challenging that first year. Kids teased and mocked her accent. They called her *little white girl* and wouldn't allow her in any of their cliques.

That first month, Rahab came home from school every day black and blue with bruises. The schoolyard kids or neighborhood kids, depending upon where she was, trapped her into scuffles.

"A fight, a fight...a negro and a white," they teased. "The black don't win we all jump in," they chanted, encircling her along with a challenger or challengers.

Not one to back down from a fight, and knowing Minton threatened to beat her if she didn't fight to win,

Rahab fought for her life. The kids quickly caught on and left her alone. She earned respect amongst her peers, but the neighborhood adults still had their reservations.

Heads turned, ears perked, and lips whispered about Puah's secret daughter.

"You sure she ain't Minton's long-lost daughter?" People questioned, willing to accept a man abandoning his child over a woman.

"How could a mother leave her child for so long and start a whole new family. She's trifling," they assumed of Puah, who was not big on making nice with nosy neighbors.

In the days, months, and years to follow, Rahab transitioned into picking up all of Puah's slack in responsibilities from cooking meals to taking care of her siblings. Even though a child, Rahab lovingly cares for them just as Lotti would have done.

The modest ranch-style home, smelling of lavender and rosemary oil, is in shipshape from top to bottom. From the surface, everything appears copacetic, but behind closed doors, the handsome, well-polished family is falling apart. Held together with broken hearts, forgotten dreams, and painful memories, the house of pain on Charlotte Street soon collapses.

TO BE CONTINUED...

For more of your favorite characters subscribe to www.authorjcmiller.com for **'Between The Scenes'** (Deleted verses from I Am Rahab: A Novel).

Be sure to pre-order your copy of,
I Am Rahab: A Novel - Part Two, coming soon!

J.C. MILLER

Made in the USA
Columbia, SC
09 November 2019